VOLUME 1

BAAN MARRUNG

THE LEGEND OF MARRA'KAI

Noah woke before the kookaburras, same as always.

Dew soaked his feet as he padded out of the family hut and onto the bush track that felt more like a hallway than a forest

 Gum leaves whispered overhead. Somewhere in the dark, a magpie gave a sleepy grumble that sounded exactly like it was telling him to go back to bed.

"Can't," Noah murmured. "River's waiting."

The earth felt different under his toes today—warmer, like a hidden fire running just beneath the roots. He paused, pressing his palm to the soil. A tiny shiver climbed up his arm, not scary, just... awake.

Big Red was already at the clearing, tail flicking, joey half-asleep beside him.

Wally the wombat snored in a dirt pile he swore was "structurally important," and Frankie the frill-neck hung upside-down from a low branch for absolutely no reason.

"You're late," Frankie said, blinking.

"Sun's not even up yet," Noah shot back.

Steve the emu stalked in behind him, all legs and attitude. "Land woke him," Steve said. "Same as it woke me."

Noah rolled his eyes, but his hand stayed pressed to the ground.

The first threads of sunlight wove through the gums as Noah followed the familiar curve of the track. Every step felt like walking through someone else's dream—soft, slow, humming with life beneath the soil.

Steve marched beside him, neck high, chest puffed out.

"You know," the emu said, "if I wasn't here, you'd be lost. Completely directionless. Hopeless, even."

"I've lived here my whole life," Noah replied. "Pretty sure I know the way."

"Instinct is not direction," Steve countered, strutting harder.

Frankie bounded ahead, leaping from rock to rock with theatrical flips. "Ignore him, mate! Emus get dramatic when they haven't had breakfast."

Big Red hopped past them with Little Red Half-asleep bouncing alongside, ears flicking. Wally trudged behind, dragging a stick twice his size.

"That your walking stick?" Noah asked.

Wally shook his head. "No. Defense stick."

"Against what?"

"Everything."

The bush shifted subtly as Noah walked—grass leaning, dust swirling in a lazy spiral. He didn't notice anymore, not really. It was like breathing. The land just... moved with him.

When the river finally came into view, glimmering cool blue under the rising sun, Noah stopped and exhaled. The water always felt like the world's first greeting.

Noah spent most mornings exactly like this

— cross-legged beside Steve, studying the tiniest creatures as if they held the secrets of the world.

He didn't know why the emu watched bugs with the same intensity as a man reading sacred law, but Noah had learned early that Steve had his own strange way of thinking.

"See that?" Noah whispered, pointing at the beetle rolling a ball of dirt twice its size.

Steve lowered his long neck and blinked. Then he gave a small grunt of approval — the sort of sound elders made when someone said something wise.

Big Red stretched out behind them with a lazy groan, Little Red curled against his Dad's warm belly. The air smelled of eucalyptus and damp soil. A perfect morning.

But soon, something odd happened.

The wind shifted. Only for a second — a tiny swirl of dust lifting around Noah's shoulder and dancing in the air. Noah didn't even notice. But Steve did. His feathers puffed, head snapping toward Noah as if he'd felt something ancient stir.

"You alright, mate?" Noah asked.

Steve stared at him for a long, still moment.

Then, very slowly, the emu nodded.

Noah grinned. "Good. C'mon, race ya to the creek!"

He took off running.
The land seemed to follow.

The creek was Noah's favourite place in the whole world. Cool water, smooth stones, and the smell of minty river plants drifting on the breeze. He leapt straight in without hesitation, the splash echoing through the trees.

"Too slow, Steve!" Noah shouted.

Steve bolted after him, legs flailing in all directions. He hit the water like a runaway wheelbarrow, sending a tidal wave across the creek. Noah was drenched instantly.

"Ohhh you muppet!" Noah laughed.

Steve made a proud rumbling noise — the emu version of yeah, take that. Big Red watched from the bank, ears twitching, looking entirely unimpressed with the chaos.

Little Red hopped beside him, copying Noah's splashing with tiny kicks that barely sent ripples out. That's when it happened again.

As Noah sprinted through the water, the ripples behind him glowed — just a faint shimmer, barely a breath long. But it wasn't sunlight. It wasn't reflection. It was something else entirely.

Steve froze mid-splash, feathers raised. His eyes locked on Noah, wide and alert.

Noah slowed. "Oi... what's wrong with you?"

Steve didn't answer — not with noise anyway. He stepped closer, cautiously, like approaching something sacred. The wind shifted again, swirling gently around Noah's ankles.

He didn't feel different.
 But Steve knew.

Something was waking.

Noah flopped onto a flat rock beneath the gum tree, rubbing at his hair with a grin. "Mate, you looked like a busted gum nut trying to run just then."

Steve didn't laugh.
 Didn't even blink.

He stepped closer, slow and deliberate, lowering his long neck until his eyes were level with Noah's. There was something intense in them — something Noah had never seen before.

"What?" Noah said, half-laughing. "You look like you're about to tell me bad news."

A breeze drifted through the clearing, swirling dry leaves in a neat little circle around Noah's feet. He didn't notice. But Steve did. The emu's feathers shivered.

Big Red's ears pricked high. Even Little Red stopped fidgeting.

Steve finally made a low, rumbling sound — not silly, not playful.
 Respectful.
 Almost... afraid.

Noah frowned. "Hey... what's wrong? You're scarin' me now."

Steve nudged him once in the chest with the tip of his beak. Not hard. Gentle. Testing something unseen.

Noah felt a thump beneath his skin — like a second heartbeat.

He didn't know it yet.
 But Steve did.

The land had begun marking its chosen.

The walk back to camp felt different.

Noah had Little Red perched on his shoulders, the joey squeaking happily as Noah bounced with each step. Big Red trailed behind, casting long shadows across the track.

 But Steve... Steve stayed close, eyes flicking between the path and Noah like he was guarding something unseen.

"You're acting weird," Noah muttered, nudging the emu with an elbow. "If you start talkin' in riddles like Djama, I'm out."

Steve let out a low "hrmmmph," but didn't joke back — not his usual sharp humour.
 It made Noah frown.

The campfire smoke curled into the twilight sky ahead. Children were already gathering, laughing, pushing each other, finding spots around the flames. Elder Djama sat with his carved staff across his lap, eyes closed, humming a deep, old tune that made the air thicken.

"Story time again," Noah said, trying to shake the unease. "Bet Djama's gonna tell the Marrakai legend for the millionth time."

Steve stiffened.

Noah didn't see it.
 Didn't notice the way Steve's feathers quivered — or how his steps slowed at the name.

Because Noah had no idea yet.
 No clue that tonight's story would begin tying his fate...
 directly to Steve's.

By the time Noah and the others reached camp, the children were already gathered tight around the fire.

Sparks drifted upward like tiny stars, and the smell of roasted damper hung sweet in the air.

Noah plopped down beside the flames, Little Red curling into his lap.

Big Red settled behind them, one massive paw resting protectively on the ground. The warmth felt good, grounding — pulling Noah out of whatever strange mood Steve had been in.

Djama opened his eyes slowly, as if waking from a long, heavy dream.
The chatter around the fire died immediately.

"Tonight," the Elder said, voice low and deep, "we speak of the old world... and the spirit who watched over it."

Noah grinned. "Here we go. Marrakai story again."

A few kids giggled. Someone elbowed him.
But Steve didn't laugh.

He lingered at the edge of the light, half-hidden, feathers tight against his body. Noah noticed him then — the stiff posture, the uneasy stare fixed on Djama's staff.

Djama's gaze drifted toward the emu for a heartbeat too long.

"Listen well," the Elder continued, tapping the earth.
"For some spirits walk closer than you think."

Djama shifted, letting the fire crackle and settle before he spoke again. The whole camp felt like it held its breath. Even the wind seemed to pause at the tree line.

"Long before our time," Djama began, voice deep and smooth, "the land was guarded by a watcher... a spirit born from storm and sky."

A few of the younger kids squealed with excitement.
 Noah smirked. He'd heard this story a hundred times — or so he thought.

But tonight... Djama's voice carried something heavier.

"He was called Marrakai," the Elder continued, gripping his staff, "the one who walked between worlds. Friend to the strong, shield to the weak, and wrath to the wicked."

The fire popped loudly, making several kids jump.

 Steve didn't move at all.

Noah glanced back at the emu.

 Steve's eyes weren't on the fire or Djama — they were fixed on the smoke swirling upward, brow furrowed as if seeing something no one else could.

Djama's voice softened.

"And some say... Marrakai never truly left."

Noah frowned.

He didn't know why, but the back of his neck prickled — a quiet feeling that tonight's version of the story was not just a story.

Djama lifted his staff, tapping it once against the packed dirt.
A hush fell so deep Noah could hear Big Red breathing behind him.

"The land is not silent," Djama said.

"It remembers. It watches. And when darkness rises…"

He paused, letting the fire roar up as if answering him. "…it chooses."

The kids looked around nervously.
Even Noah felt something tighten in his chest.

Djama drew a slow breath.
"Marrakai was not just a spirit of the storms. He was guide, mentor, protector. He walked beside the young ones of old, teaching them to hear the heartbeat of Country."

Little Red pressed closer to Noah.
Big Red wrapped his tail around them both protectively.

"And though the old stories faded," Djama continued, eyes reflecting gold, "some say he still watches the brave. The different. The ones who carry the land in their blood."

Noah swallowed hard. That strange prickling crawled up his spine again.

He looked back at Steve.

The emu wasn't looking at him…
He was staring directly at Djama — feathers raised, eyes wide, as if the Elder's words struck some buried truth.

Djama's voice dropped low.

"Tomorrow… the young ones begin their path."

The fire slowly settled into glowing embers as families drifted back to their shelters.

The night grew cooler, the sky layered with stars. Noah stretched his arms over his head and let out a long yawn.

"That was a long story," he muttered.

Steve scoffed. "Long? That bloke only scratched the surface. If he told the real version, we'd still be there next week."

Noah laughed, nudging him with his elbow. "Real version? Since when do you know anything about old spirit legends?"

Steve's feathers puffed slightly. "Mate… I know things. Important things. Mysterious things."

"Yeah, sure." Noah grinned. "Like how to steal everyone's damper."

Little Red hopped after them with a squeaky chirp. Noah reached down to pat his head, smiling as Big Red lumbered protectively behind the joey.

But as they walked toward their sleeping spot, Noah glanced back at Djama.

The Elder stood alone beside the fire pit, eyes raised to the stars as if reading messages written across the sky.

In a few years time, Noah will undertake the Marrakai ceremony — the ancient coming-of-age rite.

Djama Still tells the story of The legeng of Marra'kai today...

CHAPTER 2
STORY TIME

And today, Noah is on the verge of The Marra'kai ceremony which is just days away..

The sun had barely slipped behind the gum trees when Djama called everyone closer to the central fire.

Tonight wasn't just any story night — the air buzzed with something older, something expectant.

Noah squeezed into the front row between Steve and a few younger kids. He was halfway through stealing someone's chunk of damper when a soft voice said:

"Leave some for the rest of us, Noah."

He froze. Kirra stepped into the firelight, basket in hand, eyes warm and teasing. Noah tried his best to play it cool — but his stomach did a weird flip that had nothing to do with food.

Kirra lowered herself beside him, placing the basket between them. "You always sit in the best spot," she said.

"Yeah, well... perks of being tall?" Noah tried. It came out awkward. Steve snorted.

Djama lifted his staff, and the fire roared higher. The chatter faded instantly.

"Tonight," the Elder began, voice strong and steady, "we speak of the spirit who walked between worlds... the one who shaped the path before us."

Kirra leaned closer, whispering, "Marrakai story again?" Noah nodded — but something in Djama's eyes made him feel this version would be different.

Very different.

Djama waited until the last family settled before he spoke. The fire crackled sharply, as if it, too, wanted everyone's attention.

"Long ago," he said, voice low and steady, "before the rivers carved their paths and before the gum trees reached the sky... the worlds were not separate."

Noah felt Kirra shift beside him. She'd placed the basket between them, and the smell of fresh damper drifted up like a warm invitation. He pretended not to notice .Steve noticed everything.

The emu lowered his long neck, whispering, "He's starting with the old version. This is the one that matters."

Noah shot him a look. "How would you know?"

Steve didn't answer. His feathers only tightened.

Djama lifted his staff. The feather tips glowed softly.

"In those days," the Elder continued, "beings of sky and storm walked beside us. Some guided. Some protected. Some warned."

As he spoke, the smoke above the fire twisted — just slightly — into the shape of a wing.

Kirra leaned close, whispering, "Did you see that?"

Noah swallowed.

Djama's voice dropped low, steady as the earth beneath them.

"In the beginning, the sky was loud," he said. "Storms had voices. Winds carried warnings. And one spirit stood between them all — guiding the young, shielding the land."

The fire cracked sharply. Sparks leapt upward like startled birds.

Kirra's eyes widened. Noah felt her arm brush his — and for a moment, he forgot to breathe.

Djama continued, "He was called Marra'kai. Born of thunder. Winged by the storm. His footsteps shaped the mountains, and his breath stirred the oceans. But most of all…" Djama glanced across the circle, meeting the eyes of each child.

"…he watched over those destined to protect the land."

Steve stiffened. His feathers rose as if an invisible wind had passed straight through him.

Noah frowned.

"Steve? You good?" he whispered.

The emu didn't answer. His gaze was locked on the smoke above the fire.

And as Noah followed his stare, he saw it — for just a heartbeat.

A pair of glowing, storm-lit eyes staring back.

Then the smoke shifted, and they were gone.

Djama's voice gained a quiet strength, as though each word carried the weight of countless generations.

"Marra'kai did not walk above us," the Elder said. "He walked with us. When danger rose, he rose. When our people were lost, he guided their steps. When the land cried out, he answered."

The fire pulsed — a deep, thunder-like thump.

Noah felt it in his chest.

Kirra's eyes shimmered with the reflection of swirling smoke, her breath catching slightly as she watched the shapes twist above them.

Djama lifted his staff and traced a slow circle in the air. The smoke responded, coiling into a spiral.

"Yet even a spirit born from storm could not watch every shadow," Djama continued softly.

"For there were forces that sought to break the world apart... forces that hid behind mist and silence."

A ripple ran through Steve. His gaze snapped to the distant tree line. Noah noticed. "Steve?" he whispered.

The emu didn't blink. "The shadows he's talking about... they weren't stories."

Before Noah could ask what he meant, Djama's staff struck the ground. The fire roared upward.

And the smoke above them shifted into the unmistakable outline of wings — enormous and unfolding.

Djama's tone shifted — softer now, but heavier, like the weight of the sky was in his voice.

"Where light walks," he said, "shadow always follows. And though Marra'kai shielded our people, there were spirits that did not belong to this land... spirits with faces pale as mist." A murmur rippled through the children. Even the adults leaned in.

Noah felt a chill crawl up his spine despite the heat of the fire.

Kirra hugged her knees, eyes fixed on the swirling smoke.

Steve lowered his head slowly. "Here it comes..." he muttered.

Djama pointed his staff toward the sky. "They came silently. Watching. Searching. Not yet seen... but always near."

In the curls of smoke above, thin white shapes flickered — figures with no features, drifting like ghosts.

Noah blinked hard. "Did you—?" Kirra nodded. "I saw it."

Steve whispered, "Those aren't spirits. Not the kind he means." But before Noah could ask what he meant, Djama tapped his staff against the ground.

"Tomorrow," the Elder said, "you begin learning to see what walks unseen."

Noah swallowed.

He didn't know it yet...

But tomorrow night would be the beginning of everything.

A beginning under the midnight sky.

Djama exhaled slowly, letting the weight of the moment settle over the camp. Even the fire seemed to quiet as he lowered his staff, its glow softening.

"Where Marra'kai guarded the land," Djama said, "these others... watched from places beyond the wind. They came in silence. Always hidden. Always waiting."

A shiver ran through the circle.

Kirra tugged her knees closer, voice barely a whisper. "Why would spirits watch us?"

Djama's gaze shifted toward the horizon. "Because not all spirits seek to guide. Some seek to claim."

Noah felt his stomach twist. Something about the Elder's tone felt too real — not like a story at all.

Steve lowered his head, feathers trembling. "He's talking about them," the emu muttered. "The pale ones. The ones who walk wrong."

"What do you mean, wrong?" Noah whispered.

Steve didn't answer. The fire popped sharply, and the smoke twisted sideways, stretching into long winged shapes — but mixed within them, Noah saw blurred pale outlines like figures drifting through the mist.

Djama continued, voice lower than before. "Tomorrow's ceremony will open your eyes, Noah. You must be ready."

Noah swallowed hard.

He wasn't sure he wanted to see what walked unseen.

Djama's tone changed again — softer, but filled with an ancient strength that made Noah's skin prickle.

"Marra'kai did more than guard our people," the Elder said.

"He watched for those who would rise after him. Those born not from storm... but from the land itself."

Noah frowned slightly. "Born... from the land?" he whispered to himself.

Kirra must have heard him. She glanced sideways, studying him for a moment before returning her gaze to Djama.

The Elder pointed his staff toward the swirling smoke above. It responded instantly, condensing into the faint shape of a great eagle spirit — wings spread, chest glowing like a hidden sun.

"In every generation," Djama continued, "one child carries the echo of Marra'kai's fire. Not his power... but his purpose. A guardian meant to stand between the world and the shadows that seek it."

A few children gasped softly. Steve stiffened. Noah felt the emu's feathers brush his back, trembling with something like recognition. Djama's gaze swept the circle, then lingered briefly — intentionally — on Noah.

"And one day," the Elder said, "that guardian will rise when the land calls for him."

Noah's heart thudded once, hard.

He didn't know why.

Djama's voice rose, not in volume, but in depth — a sound layered with the echoes of those who told this tale before him.

"In the time of storms," he said, "Marra'kai walked the land not as a master... but as a teacher. He showed our ancestors how to read the wind, how to follow the stars, how to listen when the land whispered."

The smoke above the fire twisted gracefully, shaping into vast wings that swept across imagined horizons.

"He taught them strength," Djama continued, "but also balance. For power without balance invites darkness."

Steve shifted, unusually still. Noah glanced back, noticing a strange intensity in his friend's posture.

Djama traced a line through the air. The smoke parted, revealing a glowing ember-like shape — a tiny spark at the heart of the wings.

"And so," the Elder said, "Marra'kai placed a piece of his storm-fire into the world. Not in the sky... not in the rivers... but in us."

Noah blinked, confused yet drawn in.

Kirra whispered, "Us?" Djama nodded slowly.

"In one child, every generation. One spirit-fire. One future guardian."

The spark in the smoke pulsed — faint, but unmistakably alive.

Djama's staff lifted slowly, as though pulled upward by the story itself.

"When the land was young," he said, "Marra'kai shaped it not with force… but with purpose. Every river he carved was a pathway. Every mountain he raised was a shield. Every forest he grew was a promise — that our people would always have a home."

The smoke above twisted, blooming into towering mountains and sweeping plains.

"But even as he shaped the world," Djama continued, "Marra'kai saw what hid beyond the horizon. He knew shadows would one day reach for this land. Shadows not born from our world… but drifting from far places, seeking a foothold."

Noah felt a cold pulse run down his spine.

Kirra whispered, "The pale spirits…" Djama nodded without looking at her.

"And so Marra'kai left more than his teachings," the Elder said. "He left a spark. A spark to rise when the shadows returned."

The ember-shaped glow in the smoke flared bright — then dimmed, hovering directly above Noah. Steve inhaled sharply. Djama's gaze followed the ember.

"The spirit-fire chooses," he said softly.

"And it is nearly time for it to awaken."

The final ember collapsed inward with a soft hiss. Djama lowered his staff, the glowing feather dimming to a gentle pulse.

"And so," he said, voice carrying across the still camp, "each generation waits. For the land will call again when the shadows return. And one will rise with the storm-fire in his blood. One chosen not by birth... but by spirit."

Noah's breath caught.

The ember-shaped glow within the smoke drifted downward — slowly, deliberately — until it hovered above the circle. Above him.

Steve's feathers lifted in a slow ripple.

Kirra noticed Noah tense. "Hey," she whispered, "you okay?" He wasn't sure.

Djama's eyes met his — ancient, steady, filled with a knowing that made Noah's heart pound.

"The world shifts tonight," the Elder said softly. "Tomorrow begins the seeing. And soon... the choosing."

The smoke faded. The fire sank. Families quietly stood and drifted back to their shelters, speaking in low, uncertain murmurs.

But Noah remained still. Kirra placed a gentle hand on his arm. Steve stepped closer, unusually quiet. Because all three of them felt it:

Tonight, the story had changed.

Tomorrow, everything else would.

CHAPTER 3
MIDNIGHT
SECRETS

Noah didn't usually sneak away after story nights — but something about the way the firelight faded, the way Djama's voice lingered in his mind, made the world feel too loud to sleep. And when he saw Kirra walking toward the beach, basket in hand, he somehow found himself following.

Steve trotted behind with exaggerated stealth, every step a loud crunch in the sand. Big Red lumbered after them, half-awake, mumbling something about "midnight snacks."

The moon hung bright above the water, casting silver across Kirra's face.

She laughed softly as Steve tripped over a seashell. "Your emu's not very subtle."

"He's not my emu," Noah said quickly. "He just... appears.

" "Protection detail," Steve whispered proudly.

They sat near a small driftwood fire Noah built, the flames low and warm.

Kirra hugged her knees, watching the waves. "Djama's story... it felt different tonight. Like he was talking to you."

Noah swallowed. "Yeah... I felt that too." The night breeze cooled. The fire crackled.

Then Kirra froze. "Noah," she whispered, pointing toward the shoreline.

A shape stood in the mist. Tall. Motionless. Wrapped in a red coat. Its face pale as moonlight.

And staring straight at them.

The night felt different now — heavier somehow, like the tide itself was waiting.

Noah poked at the driftwood fire, watching sparks float up into the moonlight.

Kirra had barely spoken since she noticed the shape in the mist, her eyes flicking back to the shoreline again and again.

"Probably nothing," Noah said, though his voice betrayed him.

"Nothing doesn't stand still like that," Kirra whispered.

Steve leaned toward them. "Statistically, mist does not stare."

Big Red grunted. "Mist can do whatever it wants. I'm not judging."

A soft breeze swept across the sand, carrying the smell of salt and something colder — something that didn't belong.

Kirra hugged her arms. "Djama always says the beach remembers everything. Good and bad."

Noah swallowed, glancing at the water. "Do you think he meant… tonight?" The mist shifted along the shoreline, dragging low across the sand. Still no shape. Still no face.

But Noah felt it now — a presence. Watching. Waiting.

Steve stepped closer, feathers tight. "I don't like this," he muttered.

Neither did Noah.

A quiet crackle from the fire snapped

Noah's attention back to the shoreline. The mist had thickened fast — too fast.

It pushed along the sand like cold breath, weaving between driftwood and seaweed, swallowing the moonlight.

Kirra leaned closer. "Noah... it wasn't my imagination. Something was standing there."

Steve stepped forward, unusually silent. "I still vote we leave. Preferably fast."

Big Red shuffled behind them, tail twitching. "Yeah, I'm with the bird. Midnight is a terrible time for surprises."

Noah squinted into the mist. "I didn't see anything clear. Just... a shape."

Kirra hugged her arms, eyes locked on the shifting fog. "It felt like it was watching us."

A cold breeze swept across the beach, carrying a faint, unfamiliar scent — metal? Smoke? Something foreign.

Noah felt his chest tighten.

The mist parted for half a heartbeat. A vertical silhouette — tall, human-like — stood at the far edge of sight.

Then it vanished.

Steve exhaled shakily. "Nope. Definitely not mist."

The mist didn't move like mist anymore. It crawled. Slow. Intentional.

Noah rose halfway, his heart thudding in his ears. "Kirra... get back."

Steve stepped in front of them, wings slightly outstretched. His voice was low, tight. "Nobody panic. But also — panic."

Big Red crouched beside Noah, trembling. "I told you midnight was cursed."

Kirra grabbed Noah's wrist. "Noah, look!"

The mist along the shoreline twisted, folding inward like two hands parting a curtain. A hollow space opened — an archway of pale fog, leading deeper into the darkness. Noah's breath hitched. Nothing stood inside the opening. But something felt there.

Watching.

Waiting.

A sudden gust swept over the beach, cold enough to force a shiver through all of them. The driftwood fire sputtered, shrinking until only embers glowed.

Steve whispered, voice shaking, "That's not a natural formation. Something is shaping it." Noah's throat tightened. "Should we run?"

Kirra didn't answer. Her eyes were locked on the mist. The archway pulsed once — like a heartbeat.

Then a tall shadow slid behind the fog, just out of sight.

The night held its breath.

And so did they.

The archway of mist did not close. It filled.

A shape stepped into the hollow space — not with footsteps, but with a slow, sliding certainty, as if it had always been there and was only now choosing to be seen.

Noah's breath caught.

A tall figure stood within the mist, wrapped in a long red coat that fluttered without wind. Its face was pale — too pale — features blurred like charcoal smudged by a shaking hand.

Two hollow, white glints stared out where eyes should have been. Kirra's fingers dug into the sand

. "Noah," she whispered, "that's not... that's not one of ours."

Big Red pressed closer to him, trembling so hard Noah could feel it through his leg. Steve didn't move at all.

"That," the emu said quietly, "is what Djama means by 'the ones who walk wrong.'"

The figure did not step forward. It simply watched.

The waves behind it rolled in silence, their sound swallowed by the thick fog. The world felt distant, muted, like they were seeing through someone else's dream.

Noah's heart pounded.

For the first time in his life, he wished Djama's stories had just been stories. Because tonight, the pale spirit in the red coat was real.

And it knew they were there.

Noah took a shaky step backward, instinct pulling him toward the dunes. "Kirra, move," he whispered, trying to sound brave — failing completely.

Kirra didn't move. Her eyes were locked on the pale face in the mist.

"Noah... it's not alive. It's not— it's not moving like a person."

Steve didn't take his eyes off the figure. "Because it isn't one. Whatever that is... it remembers walking, but it doesn't remember how."

A chill ran down Noah's spine. "How do you even know that?"

Steve didn't answer — which scared Noah more than anything.

The figure flickered. Not forward — not backward — but sideways, like a reflection caught in shifting water.

Big Red whimpered, pressing himself flat to the sand. "Please tell me we're running now."

The mist around the figure pulsed once, and a faint echo — like a distant, broken breath — drifted across the beach.

Kirra clutched Noah's arm. "It's trying to... form something."

More shapes wavered deeper in the mist. Pale limbs. Long coats. Hollow faces. Steve stepped back toward Noah and Kirra. "We're leaving. Now."

And for the first time, Noah didn't argue.

Something ancient and wrong was waking on the shoreline.

They moved quickly, half-stumbling through the sand as the mist writhed behind them.

"Don't look back," Noah said — but his voice cracked, and Kirra knew he already had.

Steve walked backward in front of them, his long legs somehow graceful in panic. "Keep moving. Keep moving. Keep moving," he muttered like a mantra.

Big Red hopped in jittery bursts. "This is bad. This is really bad. Midnight is cursed. I knew it."

Kirra finally risked a glance over her shoulder.

The red-coat figure still stood there.

Only now its head was tilted — too far — like it was trying to understand what it was seeing.

"Noah..." she whispered. "It's watching us leave."

The mist swelled around the figure, folding over its shape until only the pale face remained — floating, unblinking. A cold pulse rolled through the air, raising goosebumps on Noah's arms. Steve hissed.

"It's not following. It's... learning."

That didn't make Noah feel any better. They crested the dune, the figure finally slipping out of sight. The ocean's roar returned, but it sounded wrong — stretched thin, hollow. Kirra clutched Noah's hand.

"We need to tell Djama," she said.

Noah nodded.

Because whatever that thing was... it wasn't done with them.

They didn't stop until they reached the dunes. Only when the sand leveled beneath them did Noah finally let himself breathe. His chest heaved, heart slamming against his ribs.

Kirra placed a shaky hand on his shoulder. "Noah... what was that thing?"

He shook his head. "I don't know. But Djama will."

Steve stood at the edge of the dune, staring down at the fog-wrapped shoreline. "It didn't follow," he murmured. "It stayed. Like it was waiting for something."

Big Red curled close to the group, trembling. "Waiting for what? We're delicious. That's what."

Noah managed a weak breath. "Red... now's not the time."

But even as he said it, he looked back toward the mist — half-expecting to see the pale face staring up at them. All he saw was the fog shifting in broken, unnatural movements.

Kirra swallowed. "We have to tell Djama right now. Tonight. Before... before anything else happens."

Steve nodded sharply. "Agreed. And we're sticking together. No wandering. No midnight strolls."

Noah straightened, gathering what courage he had left.

"Let's go."

They turned toward the camp — unaware that the mist below pulsed softly, as if breathing.

Branches whipped at Noah's arms as he pushed through the narrow trail, the camp lights still far ahead. The night felt wrong — too still, too cold.

"Keep moving," Steve urged, stepping lightly despite his size. "Don't slow down."

Kirra kept close to Noah, her breath tight. "Do you think it's still there?"

Noah didn't answer.

He didn't want to think about the pale face waiting in the mist. Big Red hopped faster to keep up.

"I swear something's behind us," he whispered, glancing back every few steps. "If I see that coat again, I'm gone."

A rustle echoed from the trees. All four froze. Noah turned slowly — expecting the mist. But it was only wind pushing through leaves.

Still, the fear didn't fade. Steve stepped between Noah and the dark. "Whatever that thing was... it wasn't just looking at us. It was looking through us."

Kirra shivered. "Djama has to know. He'll understand this. He has to."

Noah nodded, forcing his legs to move again. "We're almost there. Just a little—"

A low, distant pulse drifted from the direction of the beach. They all stopped.

The mist was calling.

But they turned away — hurrying toward the only person who might have answers.

They broke through the last line of trees and into the glow of the campfires.

The warmth hit Noah like a wave, but it did nothing to steady his racing heart.

Djama turned at the sound of their footsteps. His eyes narrowed the moment he saw their faces. "What has happened?"

Noah tried to speak, but Kirra beat him to it. "Djama... there was something on the beach. In the mist. A man — or a spirit — or something that looked like one."

Djama's expression shifted, ancient caution rising behind his eyes. "Describe it."

"It wore a red coat," Noah said, voice shaking. "And its face... it wasn't right."

Steve stepped forward. "It wasn't walking. It was remembering walking." Djama froze. For a long, heavy moment, he said nothing. Then:

"You all stay here. No wandering. No fires alone. No stepping beyond the circle of the camp." His voice was firm, almost trembling beneath its weight.

Kirra touched Noah's arm. "He knows something."

Djama nodded once, solemn. "I will speak to the spirits tonight. There is danger in the wind... but perhaps also a protector." His eyes lingered on Noah.

Noah swallowed hard.

Whatever they saw on the beach... it had changed everything.

CHAPTER 4 –
DJAMA'S WARNING

The fire crackled softly as Noah and Kirra stood before Djama, their breaths still uneven from running. The night around the camp felt different now — too still, too expectant. Families gathered at a distance, whispering, watching the three of them with wide, unsettled eyes.

Djama planted his staff beside the fire.
"Tell me again," he said quietly. "Every detail."

Noah tried, but the words tangled inside him.

Kirra stepped forward first. "Djama... it wasn't just mist. It shaped itself. Like a man. Like something trying to be one." She held her basket tightly as if it might steady her shaking hands.

Djama's eyes narrowed. "Its coat was red?"

Noah nodded. "Dark red. And its face... it didn't look alive."

Steve shuddered. "Or dead. It was... something-between."

A hush fell. Even the wind seemed to pull back.

Djama stared into the fire, its glow reflecting in his deep-set eyes.

"Long ago," he murmured, "spirits warned us of beings who walk wrong — neither from this world nor the next."

He looked at Noah then, gaze heavy with meaning.
"If such a one has returned... the land will tremble. And a protector must rise."

Noah felt his chest tighten.
He didn't know why — but Djama was looking at him.

Djama said nothing more at the fire. Instead, he turned sharply and motioned for Noah and Kirra to follow.

 The camp parted around them, families stepping back as if the shadows themselves had weight. Noah felt their eyes on him—fearful, searching—but Djama's stare on his back was heavier.

They walked toward the darker edge of the camp, the night closing in as the warm firelight faded behind them. Steve and Big Red followed tightly, unusually quiet.

"Djama…" Kirra whispered, but he lifted a hand for silence.

The trees opened to a small clearing where the earth was bare and circular—Noah remembered seeing Djama come here alone at night, always returning with answers he never fully explained.

Djama stepped to the center and planted his staff into the soil. The feather at its tip flickered faintly, as though sensing something in the air.

"Now," Djama said, voice low, "tell me exactly what you saw. No fear. No guessing."

Noah swallowed hard. "It looked like mist shaped like a man. Wearing a red coat. Eyes… like empty light."

Kirra nodded. "It felt wrong. Like it wasn't supposed to be here."

Djama's jaw tightened.

"Then the spirits must speak tonight."

Djama lowered himself to one knee at the center of the clearing, the same silent place he had used for every spirit-calling since Noah was small enough to sit in his lap. The air felt heavier here, as though unseen hands pressed down upon the land.

Noah, Kirra, Steve, and Big Red stood close together at the edge of the circle. None of them dared speak. Even Steve's feathers stayed flat and still.

Djama pressed his palm to the earth. The ground was cool, but beneath it Noah sensed something shifting—like breath moving through soil.

"Ancestors," Djama murmured, "hear me. The children have seen a walker of wrong places. Show me what stirs in the mist. Show me what comes for our people."

A thin ribbon of smoke rose from the ground, drifting upward in spirals.

Kirra clutched her basket tightly. Big Red whined low in his throat.

Djama's eyes fluttered shut. His breath grew slow. The smoke twisted, forming shapes—half-faces, hands, shadows clinging to one another.

Then Djama inhaled sharply, as if struck.

Noah stepped forward. "Djama? What do you see?"

Djama's voice trembled. "A warning... and a name carried in fire. One who must rise."

The smoke thickened as Djama's breaths deepened. Each exhale sent new spirals into the air, and each spiral twisted into something more defined — an outline, a wing, a pale drifting shape that vanished before fully forming.

Kirra clutched Noah's arm. "It's reacting to him... like it knows."

Steve stepped forward cautiously. "Or like it remembers him." Djama's eyes snapped open.

"No," he whispered. "It remembers you all."

Noah's stomach dropped. The smoke above Djama suddenly folded inward, forming a single shape — the unmistakable outline of a tall figure with a long coat. The same silhouette they saw on the beach. Djama reached toward the smoke and flinched as if burned.

"These are not spirits of our land," he said, voice shaking. "They drift from far places... carried by winds not meant for this Country."

Noah felt the cold settle into his bones. "Djama... what does it want?"

Djama looked directly at him.

"It searches," he said. "For a weakness. Or for a protector yet to rise."

The wind came without warning. A sharp, cold gust cut through the clearing, scattering leaves and forcing Noah and Kirra to shield their faces. Even Steve stumbled back a step, feathers rippling in every direction.

Djama did not move. His staff glowed brighter, anchoring him to the earth as the smoke above twisted violently.

The shapes inside it no longer drifted—they lashed, collided, and warped into flashes of storm clouds and streaks of red, like torn fabric whipping through the air.

"Djama!" Noah shouted over the rising wind. Djama's voice became strained. "The land... it's speaking. The danger is not wandering. It is coming."

Kirra's grip tightened on Noah's arm. "Coming from where?" The smoke snapped downward, swirling around Djama like a living thing. He winced, eyes squeezed shut.

"From the sea," he whispered. "Carried on ships... faces pale as moonlight. Coats red as blood."

Noah's breath left him. The figure from the beach. But Djama wasn't finished.

"There is fire ahead," he said, voice breaking. "A warning. A loss... one that will change your path."

Big Red let out a small, trembling whine. And Noah felt the first crack of dread in his chest.

The wind died as suddenly as it had come, leaving the clearing heavy with silence. Djama's staff dimmed, the feather's glow fading to a soft ember. The Elder swayed where he knelt. Noah rushed forward. "Djama! Are you okay?"

Djama lifted a hand, breathing hard. "I am... here. The spirits took much to show what they did." Kirra knelt on his other side, steadying him. "What did they mean? Fire? A loss?"

Djama's eyes opened slowly—eyes older than moments before. "The land cries out... something burns where it should not."

Steve's head snapped toward the treeline. "Burns? As in... fire fire?"

Big Red whimpered, shrinking into himself. Noah swallowed. "Is it the figure from the beach? Did it cause this?" Djama shook his head weakly. "No. This fire is of this world. But its timing is no accident." He looked toward the distant horizon, where only darkness should have been.

But Noah saw it then—a faint orange shimmer, barely visible between branches. Kirra gasped. "Is that... smoke?" Djama's face tightened with sorrow.

"It is a warning," he said softly. "And someone will pay its price."

Big Red made a small, broken sound. Noah's heart dropped. Something was burning— and it was close to home.

Big Red moved before anyone else.

One moment he was crouched behind Noah, trembling; the next his ears shot upward and his whole body locked in place.

His gaze fixed on the faint orange shimmer on the horizon—no longer tiny, no longer ignorable.

"No…" Big Red whispered, voice cracking.

"No… no no no…"

Noah followed his stare. The glow was brighter now, pulsing softly against the dark sky.

Smoke—thin but real—rose in slow waves.

Kirra covered her mouth. "Djama… that's a fire."

Djama stood slowly, leaning heavily on his staff. His face was grim. "The spirits showed truth. The land is burning where it should not."

Steve stepped forward, feathers stiff. "That's toward Red's home."

Big Red let out a broken sound—half sob, half gasp—and bolted a few steps forward before stopping, shaking violently. Noah moved to his side. "Red… we'll go. We'll help."

Big Red's eyes were wide and glassy. "My family… my home…" Djama nodded, voice low but firm. "There is no time to waste."

The orange glow flickered brighter. The fire wasn't waiting.

And neither could they.

The smoke thickened as they pushed deeper into the bush, turning the cool night air hot and sharp. Noah's lungs burned, but he didn't slow. Every time Big Red stumbled, Noah forced himself faster.

Kirra wiped her eyes, coughing. "It's spreading," she managed. "Faster than it should."

Steve sprinted beside them, his long legs slicing through undergrowth. "This isn't natural," he said, feathers tight. "Fire doesn't move like this at night. Not without wind."

Djama kept pace despite leaning heavily on his staff. "The land warned us. We arrive now because we were meant to."

A cracking boom split the night—a burning tree collapsing nearby.

Big Red let out a strangled cry and bolted ahead, faster than Noah had ever seen.

"MUM! DAD! LITTLE RED!"

Noah pushed himself harder, heart pounding with dread. The sky ahead glowed bright orange now, flickering violently through the trees. Embers drifted around them like falling stars.

Kirra grabbed Noah's arm to steady herself. "We're close!"

Another thunderous crack echoed.

They burst through the final line of trees—heat slamming into them like a wall.

Big Red's home valley was an inferno.

The blazing valley stole their breath.

Flames roared through the trees, devouring everything in their path.

What had once been Big Red's peaceful home was now a wall of fire, heat radiating so fiercely that Noah had to shield his face. Big Red stumbled forward, the orange glow painting his fur in trembling highlights.

"Mum? Dad?" His voice cracked into something small and terrified. Noah grabbed his arm gently.

"Red... wait. It's not safe."

But Big Red pulled away, hopping closer to the burning clearing. Steve moved beside Noah, feathers flat and sorrowful. "This wasn't a natural fire," he said quietly. "Something —someone—started this." Djama stepped forward, planting his staff firmly. "The spirits showed this loss," he murmured. "But loss is never without meaning."

A faint cry pierced the crackle of flames.

Everyone froze.

Kirra's eyes widened. "Did you hear that?"

Another cry—small, frightened.

Big Red gasped. "LITTLE RED!"

Noah's heart leapt as Big Red sprinted toward the sound, disappearing briefly behind a smoldering fallen branch.

Then, through drifting smoke, they saw him reappear—Little Red clinging to his chest, shaking but alive. Relief washed through the group—but the fire still raged behind them, hungry and merciless.

BIG RED, NO!

Big Red held Little Red as if afraid he might vanish again. The smaller kangaroo clung to him with tiny trembling paws, burying his face in Big Red's chest.

A sound escaped Big Red—a mix of relief and heartbreak that made Noah's throat tighten.

Kirra knelt beside them, brushing ash from Little Red's fur. "You're safe now," she whispered. "You're both safe."

But they all knew safety was temporary. The fire roared behind them, devouring what remained of Big Red's home.

Trees cracked and fell, sending sparks spiraling into the sky.

Steve stood beside Noah, unusually quiet. Djama stepped forward, the glow of his staff flickering against the smoke. "There is sorr

ow tonight," he said softly. "But there is also truth."

Noah turned toward him. "What truth?"

Djama's eyes reflected the flames—old, knowing, burdened.

"The shadows that walk wrong have returned. This fire is only their beginning. And the land will need a protector—one chosen by spirit, not by chance." His gaze settled on Noah.

Kirra looked at him, breath catching.

The fire behind them roared higher, as if answering Djama's words.

And Noah felt it—deep in his chest. Something was awakening.

BAAN MARRUNG
CHAPTER 5 – INTO THE FLAMES

The fire behind them had begun to settle into a slow, angry burn, but the heat still pushed at Noah's back like a living thing.

Little Red trembled in his arms, tiny paws gripping Noah's chest.

Kirra stood close beside him, her touch steady.

Big Red hadn't moved since they'd pulled Little Red from the ashes.

He sat hunched before what had once been his home, staring into the twisted ruins as drifting ash settled across his fur.

Steve watched silently, blinking in slow disbelief.

Djama stepped forward, the glow of his staff cutting through the smoke.

"The land mourns with him," he said gently. "Tonight, fire has taken more than a home."

Noah swallowed. "What do we do now?"

Djama's eyes were heavy but certain.

"Now you stay close to one another. This sorrow is only the first shadow the spirits warned of."

Noah tightened his hold on Little Red.

Something inside him stirred in response.

The night exploded into motion.

Noah swung himself onto Steve's back before he even realized he was doing it.

The emu didn't argue—he just bolted, legs a blur, wings tucked tight as he charged toward the rising glow on the horizon.

Kirra ran beside them, clutching her basket against her chest, breath sharp, eyes locked on the fire ahead.

Djama followed behind, moving slower but purposeful, his staff glowing brighter with every step as if feeding on the danger.

Big Red bounded unevenly, Little Red cradled tightly against him. The younger kangaroo let out soft, frightened squeaks, burying himself deeper into Big Red's fur.

"Noah, wait!" Kirra called—but Noah couldn't. Something deep inside him—something old—pulled him toward the flames.

The sky above them shifted from moonlit blue to a sickly orange.

Smoke rolled low across the ground, curling around their feet. Embers drifted like fireflies, carried on the wind.

Steve skidded to a stop at the top of a ridge.

Below them, the world burned.

A wall of fire roared through the bush, swallowing trees and shadows alike.

Kirra reached Noah's side, breathless. "Djama was right... something terrible happened here."

STEVE,
LET'S MOVE!

They descended the ridge in silence—no words could rise above the roar of the burning earth below. Big Red reached the clearing first.

He stumbled to a stop, breath hitching, as the world he knew lay flattened before him. His home was gone—nothing left but black earth and the glowing ribs of fallen trees.

The air shimmered with heat, the smell of ash thick enough to taste.

Little Red whimpered softly, pressing deeper into Big Red's chest.

Noah stepped forward, his heart twisting. "Red… I'm so sorry."

Big Red didn't answer. Couldn't. His eyes were wide, hollow, reflecting the embers like dying stars.

Kirra moved to Noah's side, her voice barely a whisper. "This wasn't an accident."

Djama's staff glowed brighter, responding to the tension in the air. "Fire came swiftly. Too swiftly for the trees to warn us."

Steve swallowed hard, feathers tight against his body. "Then what caused it? Lightning? Or…"

Djama shook his head. "No storm passed here tonight."

Noah looked at the blackened ground. The heat. The pattern of destruction.

Something unnatural had happened. And the truth of it pressed against his chest, cold and heavy.

Big Red slowly lowered himself into the ash, legs folding beneath him as if the weight of his grief pressed him into the earth.

Little Red clung to his chest, tiny paws gripping his fur, trembling in short desperate bursts.

Noah stepped forward and knelt beside him, offering a steady hand on Red's shoulder.

"Hey… we're here. We're not leaving you," he whispered, voice thick with emotion.

Big Red's breath shuddered. He didn't speak—he couldn't—but the quiet sounds that escaped him were enough to break Noah's heart all over again.

Kirra moved in close, resting a gentle hand on Noah's back.

"We'll rebuild," she murmured. "Together. You won't face this alone."

Steve stood unusually still, feathers pressed flat as he stared at the scorched earth.

"This wasn't normal fire…" he said quietly.

Djama approached then, staff glowing brighter as he traced patterns in the burned soil with his fingertips. His eyes darkened.

"No," he said softly. "This was guided. Driven by a force that should not be here."

Noah felt the air around them shift. A warning laid in ash. A beginning carved by flame.

Djama crouched low, dragging his fingers gently through the blackened soil. The ash parted beneath his touch, revealing char patterns that twisted like claw marks—or something worse.

Kirra stepped forward. "Djama... what is it?"

The Elder didn't answer immediately. His staff glowed brighter, casting gold light over the strange curves scorched into the ground. Noah swallowed hard. "That doesn't look like lightning."

Steve squinted. "And trust me, I've been struck before. Purely for scientific interest."

Even Big Red managed a weak sound—half gasp, half sob—as he clutched Little Red tighter.

Djama finally spoke. "Fire should spread with the wind. But here..." He pointed to the marks. "It moved against it."

Kirra's brow furrowed. "How is that possible?"

Djama rose slowly, his expression dark. "Only if something carried it. Something that walks where it should not. Something that does not belong to this land."

Noah felt a sinking weight in his chest. "You mean... like the red-coat spirit?"

Djama's gaze met his.

"Not the same one," he said quietly. "But kin to it."

Little Red whimpered. And the forest felt suddenly colder.

Noah stepped to the edge of the clearing, eyes following the jagged burn trail that disappeared into the deeper forest.

The ground looked wrong—split, twisted, as if the fire had been pulled along by invisible hands.

Kirra came to stand beside him, her brow tight with worry. "It keeps going... all the way into the trees."

Steve lowered his long neck, staring at the trail with a seriousness Noah rarely saw on him. "Whatever did this... it didn't just burn. It searched."

Djama approached, planting his staff firmly.

The faint glow pulsed once, reflecting his troubled expression. "The spirits warned of shadows that walk where they should not. This path..." He pointed with the end of his staff.

"This is not the work of wind or storm. It is the mark of something guided by intent."

Big Red whimpered softly behind them, pulling Little Red closer. The young roo's ears twitched with every distant sound.

Noah clenched his fists. "So it's still out there."

Djama nodded slowly. "Yes. And whatever it seeks... it has not found it yet."

A cold breeze pushed through the ruined clearing. And for the first time, Noah felt the forest watching them back.

They didn't leave the clearing quickly. Grief held them there, heavy as the smoke that curled around the charred trunks. But eventually, Djama lifted his staff and nodded—softly, sorrowfully.

"It is time," he said. "The land will rest now. And so must we."

Big Red rose shakily, Little Red pressed tightly against him. The young roo was silent, eyes wide and unfocused, as if afraid the world might vanish if he blinked.

Noah moved to Big Red's side, placing a steadying hand on his arm. "We'll walk together," he said. "You're not doing this alone."

Big Red didn't trust his voice, so he only nodded.

Steve walked ahead, every rustle making him tense. "I'm just saying," he muttered, "if anything jumps out at us tonight, I'm kicking it. I don't care what it is."

Kirra managed a small, tired smile.

Djama lingered at the edge of the clearing, eyes sweeping the burn one last time. The glow of his staff dimmed, but his expression didn't soften.

"This fire," he murmured, "was not the end. It was the first sign."

Noah turned back toward him. A chill passed between them. Something dark had begun— and it was following them into the night.

Dawn crept in slowly, painting the world in pale blue as the group made their way back through the thinning forest. The fire's harsh glow no longer chased them; instead, a soft morning light stretched across the ground, touching the smoke-stained leaves with gentle color.

Big Red walked heavily, each step careful. Little Red stayed pressed to his side, eyelids drooping, overwhelmed by fear and exhaustion. Noah stayed close, ready to catch either of them if they faltered.

Kirra walked beside Noah, her hand brushing his every so often—not by accident. "He's hurting so much," she whispered.

"I know," Noah said quietly. "But we won't let him face it alone."

Steve trotted near Noah's feet, unusually subdued. "Sunrise feels different today," he muttered. "Like the world's trying to pretend nothing happened."

Djama didn't turn back, but his voice carried softly. "The world remembers. The land remembers. But morning always brings strength."

As they stepped beyond the last row of trees, the camp came into view.

Warm smoke curled from the fires. People stirred.

For a moment—just a moment—Noah let himself breathe. Because even after the flames, morning had found them.

The first villagers spotted them before they even stepped fully into the clearing.

Gasps echoed through the camp as Big Red limped forward, ash still clinging to his fur, Little Red pressed tightly against his side. Mothers pulled their children close.

Elders rose to their feet, faces lined with worry.

Noah moved ahead slightly, guiding Big Red with a steady hand. Kirra stayed close to Little Red, whispering soft comforts as his tiny body trembled.

Steve puffed himself up—not in pride, but in a protective stance Noah had only ever seen a few times. His eyes scanned the camp, daring anything else to go wrong.

Djama walked in last, the rising sun catching the edges of his staff. The glow around him dimmed softly, as though even the spirits were weary from the night.

"What happened?" a villager whispered.

Djama stepped forward. "A fire took Red's home. And something more dangerous than flame moved with it."

A ripple passed through the crowd.

Noah felt their eyes shift toward him—some with fear, others with hope.

He didn't know which frightened him more.

The land had changed during the night. And so had he.

As the sun cleared the treetops, Djama stepped into the center of the camp. The villagers formed a loose circle around him—some still waking, others already whispering about the night's disaster.

The weight of expectation settled in the air like dust.

Noah stood at the front beside Kirra, Steve, and Big Red. Little Red curled against Big Red's side, exhausted but safe. The warmth of the morning fires did little to ease the heaviness in their chests.

Djama raised his staff, the glow catching the light of dawn. Silence fell instantly.

"What happened last night," Djama began, "was not the work of a wandering fire. It was a sign. A warning carried on paths not meant for mortal feet. The shadows that walk wrong have returned to this land."

A murmur rippled through the crowd.

Djama turned his gaze toward Noah—steady, knowing. "But the spirits also showed me this: when darkness rises, the land does not stand alone. A protector will rise with it. One chosen not by birth, but by the fire in their spirit."

Noah felt the words settle into him, heavy and electric.

Kirra reached for his hand.

For the first time, Noah didn't pull away.

Whatever was coming... he would not face it alone.

CHAPTER 6 –
OUR MOB

The morning light crept slowly into the camp, pushing aside the last wisps of smoke that still clung to the cool air.

It should have felt peaceful, but instead the dawn only revealed the weight left behind by the fire.

Big Red sat near the small shelter the mob had built for him overnight.

His body curved protectively around Little Red, who pressed into his chest with trembling paws. Neither had spoken since the blaze. Big Red's usually relaxed ears hung low, his posture sagging with a grief Noah had never seen.

Noah approached with Kirra at his side. He hesitated. "Should we say something?"

Kirra squeezed his arm gently. "Say it with care. His whole world changed last night."

Nearby, Steve paced back and forth, feathers tucked tight. Wally waddled over carrying a fistful of flowers—roots, dirt, and all. Frankie groaned theatrically. "Wally... those are weeds."

Big Red blinked at the offering. A tiny breath escaped him—not quite a laugh, but not despair either.

For the first time since the flames, something shifted.

Not healed.

But hopeful.

By mid-morning, the entire mob had gathered at the charred remains of Big Red's home. No one had to be asked — they came because that was what the mob did. When one hurt, all moved.

Noah carried a woven basket filled with fresh bark sheets and tools. Kirra walked beside him, water skins slung over her shoulder. The elders were already laying down cleansing leaves, their hands steady and practiced, even as their eyes shone with quiet sorrow.

Children gathered unburnt branches. Adults sifted through the ruins for anything salvageable. Smoke curled gently through the air, carrying the scent of ash and eucalyptus.

Steve stumbled in dramatically with an armful of crooked sticks. "I'm helping! I'm VERY helpful!"

Frankie slapped a claw against his forehead. "Steve... those are the wrong sticks."

Djama watched them all with a soft, knowing expression, his staff's feather glowing faintly. "Strength is not only in the body," he murmured, mostly to Noah. "It is in how we stand for each other."

Noah nodded, feeling the truth settle deeper inside him.

Big Red lifted his head, eyes wet, as the community rebuilt around him.

For the first time since the fire... he didn't feel alone.

Big Red hadn't moved from the spot where they'd found Little Red.

He sat hunched over, long arms wrapped around the tiny joey as if letting go would break the world in half.

Little Red pressed his face tightly into Big Red's fur, trembling with each uneven breath.

Noah approached slowly, letting his footsteps crunch softly so Big Red wouldn't be startled.

"Hey... Red," Noah whispered. "We're here. All of us."

Big Red didn't look up at first. His chest rose and fell in heavy, uneven shudders. When he finally lifted his eyes, they were wet and distant.

"I couldn't save her..." he murmured, voice cracking. "I tried. I tried so hard."

Noah sank to a knee beside him. "You did everything anyone could. And Little Red... he's alive because of you."

Little Red peeked out, tiny paws gripping Noah's arm as if asking for strength he didn't yet have. Noah rubbed the joey's back gently.

Kirra stepped forward and placed a calming hand on Big Red's shoulder. "We're your mob. You're not carrying this alone."

Behind them, Steve wiped a feather under his eye. "I'm not crying," he sniffed. "It's just... smoky."

Frankie kicked him lightly. "Yeah. Very smoky."

But even Big Red managed the smallest, aching smile.

By mid-morning, the mob had moved like a single body — steady, silent, carrying both sorrow and purpose.

Noah wiped soot from his palms and helped lift a support beam into place.

The villagers guiding it exchanged nods with him, and Noah felt a strange shift inside: they trusted him. Not because he was the strongest, but because he showed up wherever he was needed.

Kirra worked nearby, laying woven grass bedding across the floor of the small shelter they were building for Big Red and Little Red.

The joey curled against her knee, blinking sleepily. When Noah paused to watch, she offered him a tired smile — one that warmed him in a way the morning sun couldn't.

Around them, the mob worked efficiently. Dave raked the ground smooth. Two aunties passed water skins down the line. Steve strutted importantly with a twig the size of a finger. "Critical reinforcement," he declared. Frankie snorted so hard he fell off a log.

For the first time since dawn, Big Red looked around — really looked — at everyone rebuilding the home he'd lost.

His voice cracked as he whispered, "Our mob…"

Noah placed a hand on his shoulder.

"We're here," he said. "All of us."

The clearing buzzed with movement, but it wasn't frantic. It was steady — the rhythm of a mob working with one heart.

Noah carried a basket of bark and tools to a growing pile near the new shelter frame. Kirra was kneeling with Little Red tucked close against her side, wiping ash gently from the joey's fur.

Big Red watched, ears still drooped, but there was a soft gratefulness in his gaze now.

Wally trudged past Noah, proudly dragging an entire bush — roots, dirt, leaves, everything. "I brought flowers," he announced.

Frankie slapped both hands over his face. "Wally, that's not flowers — that's a crime scene!"

A few nearby aunties snorted with laughter. Even Big Red's shoulders loosened.

Steve stumbled by with two water skins, nearly tripping on flat ground. "Someone warn the ground before it jumps at me," he muttered.

Noah couldn't help smiling. The heaviness from last night lifted just a little.

Djama watched from the edge of the clearing, leaning on his staff, eyes following Noah. The Elder saw what the boy didn't — how the mob's movements aligned around him, how he stepped in to help without needing to be asked.

Quietly, Djama whispered:

"He walks the path without knowing."

By late morning the rhythm of rebuilding had settled into something almost peaceful.

Noah tightened his grip as he and two uncles lifted a heavy beam into place. Their muscles strained, feet digging into the ash-stained earth. When the beam locked into its support, the uncles clapped him proudly on the back.

"You're growing strong, boy," one said.

Noah laughed softly, embarrassed — but something warm bloomed in his chest.

A few steps away, Kirra smoothed woven grasses into a soft bed for Little Red. The joey wriggled in happily, nudging her elbow.

Big Red stood nearby, still weary, still grieving, but lifting small pieces of charred wood, trying to help in any way he could.

Djama observed from the shade of a burnt eucalypt, tapping his staff lightly into the soil. A faint shimmer circled Noah's feet — drifting leaves that moved without breeze.

Kirra noticed it first. "Noah... look."

Noah glanced down, confused. The leaves stilled the moment he paid attention, falling quietly to the ground.

Djama's voice carried across the clearing. "The land knows who lifts with heart," he said. "The spirits listen."

Noah wasn't sure what that meant — but it made his pulse quicken.

He felt... different.

It had been a long, heavy morning — but by afternoon, something began to shift.

Wally waddled into the clearing dragging the largest branch anyone had ever seen him attempt. It bounced and snagged on every rock and root in its path, nearly flipping him over more than once.

Frankie marched alongside him, frill flared dramatically. "Left! No — my left, not your left! Wally, honestly, do you train to be this slow or is it a gift?"

Wally blinked. "I thought the big ones would be useful…"

"They would be if you weren't shaped like a potato!"

Noah nearly dropped the basket he was carrying with Kirra from laughing. Even Big Red huffed a tiny, broken chuckle — the first smile they'd seen on him since the night before.

Steve strutted past with far too many baskets stacked across his back. "Everyone calm down. A professional has arrived." Then he tripped over a stump, sending the baskets flying like startled birds.

The entire mob burst into gentle, much-needed laughter.

For a moment, the ash, the grief, and the warnings of spirits felt distant.

Noah exhaled, feeling the weight in his chest finally loosen.

Together… they were finding their way back.

By late afternoon, the worst of the clean-up had slowed. Voices softened.

The mob moved with tired determination rather than panic. And at the edge of the rebuilt shelter, Big Red sat unmoving, Little Red curled tightly against him.

Noah approached with steady, careful steps. "Hey... thought you two might need this." He set down a bowl of cool water and a folded leaf wrap warmed earlier by the fire.

Big Red didn't speak. His eyes stayed fixed on the horizon, shoulders low, ears barely lifting at Noah's voice. But Little Red shifted, nudging the wrap with a shaky paw before pulling it against himself.

Kirra joined Noah, spreading soft grasses into a neat bedding pile. "He's holding so much," she whispered. "Trying to be strong for Little Red."

Noah nodded. "He shouldn't have to do it alone."

Steve stepped forward, lowering his long neck in a quiet gesture of respect. "We're here, mate. All of us."

For the first time all day, Big Red's gaze moved. Slowly, heavily, he looked at Noah, at Kirra, at Steve... at his mob.

His voice cracked. "Thank you."

And in that fragile moment, the whole world seemed to pause — just long enough for healing to begin.

Night drifted in slowly, the sky shifting from gold to deep violet.

The fires glowed warm rather than frantic now, their light dancing across the faces of the weary mob.

Near the shelter, Noah and Kirra worked side by side, gently tending to Little Red.

"He's breathing easier," Kirra murmured, brushing soot from the joey's ears.

Little Red wriggled closer, pressing himself against Noah's side. Noah smiled, though his chest still felt heavy. "He's tough... just like his dad."

Kirra's hand rested briefly atop Noah's as they wrapped fresh leaves around Little Red's tiny paws. The touch was soft, unspoken — but it warmed him more than the fire ever could.

Big Red watched from a few steps away, eyes glistening in the firelight. For the first time since the flames took his home, his shoulders eased. "He trusts you," he said quietly.

Steve plopped down beside them, feathers puffed with solemn pride. "We are providing emotional stability," he declared.

Kirra laughed — a small, bright sound the mob desperately needed.

Noah looked around at the circle of people and animals gathered close, helping, supporting, healing.

For the first time all day, hope didn't feel far away.

It felt... here.

The night settled softly over the camp, the fire crackling calm and steady now. Noah and Kirra sat at its edge, neither speaking for a long time. They didn't need to. The day had said enough.

Big Red and Little Red slept peacefully in their new shelter, the rise and fall of their breaths finally steady. Wally snored upright, wobbling with each inhale. Frankie puffed out his frill and announced that he was "guarding the whole world," though he nearly toppled off the log twice.

Steve lay nearby with his eyes closed, but one cracked open whenever Noah or Kirra shifted. Subtlety wasn't his strong point.

Kirra leaned her shoulder lightly against Noah's. "You helped everyone today," she said softly.

Noah stared into the flames. "I just... didn't want him to lose everything."

"You didn't let him," she whispered. "That matters."

Across the clearing, Djama stood beneath the trees, his staff glowing with a quiet pulse. He watched Noah—not with worry, but with recognition.

The protector the spirits spoke of was no longer a distant idea.

He was sitting right here by the fire.

Noah exhaled slowly, the warmth settling into his chest.

Tomorrow, his path would begin to change.

But tonight...
he belonged to his mob.

Chapter 7 –
For Kirra

The camp had quieted as night settled in, but Noah's heartbeat felt louder than the crackle of any fire. Every step he took toward Kirra's shelter felt heavier, more real. He could still feel Kirra's shoulder against his earlier, her words echoing:

"You carry others without even knowing it."

He didn't feel like a protector. Not yet.
 But he wanted to be someone worthy of walking beside her.

Elders glanced up as he passed, their expressions unreadable but gentle. Families murmured softly, unaware of the storm inside Noah's chest. The firelight painted everything in warm gold, but his palms were cold with nerves.

Kirra sat near her father's shelter, plaiting dried leaves with steady hands. When she saw Noah approach, her breath hitched—just slightly. She didn't speak, but her eyes asked everything.

Kirra's father rose slowly. Strong. Calm. Watching Noah with the weight of generations behind his gaze.

Noah swallowed and bowed his head respectfully.

"I... I want to walk beside Kirra," he said quietly, voice steady despite the tremble inside. "If you allow it."

Behind a nearby tree, Steve whispered loudly, "HE'S DOING IT!"

Frankie shushed him with unnecessary drama.

Kirra's father said nothing yet—only studying Noah, measuring the boy before him.

And Noah held his ground.

Kirra's father stood silent for a long moment, arms crossed over his chest, eyes fixed on Noah. There was no anger in his face — only depth, memory, and the full measure of a father's responsibility.

"You speak big words for someone still finding his feet," he said at last, voice low and thoughtful.

Noah nodded. "I know. But I mean every one of them."

Kirra's breath wavered. She took a small step closer, hope flickering behind her uncertainty.

Her father's gaze shifted to her before returning to Noah. "You think walking beside my daughter is simple? That it's only about liking someone?"

"No," Noah said. "It's about honour. And work. And showing I can carry my part."

A faint smile ghosted through Kirra's father's beard — not approval, not yet, but recognition.

"You helped your mob today," he said. "Stood for them when sorrow fell. Comforted those who lost." His eyes narrowed. "But a man doesn't prove himself only in moments of fire."

Noah swallowed. "Tell me what I must do."

Behind the tree, Steve punched the air silently.

Kirra's father stepped closer, eyes hardening with ritual significance.

"Then hear me, Noah. If you want to walk beside my daughter... there is a task you must undertake."

Kirra's father placed a carved stick gently into the sand between them — a symbol of intention, of promises spoken and paths chosen.

"Noah," he said, voice steady as stone, "to walk beside my daughter, you must show more than courage in a moment of danger. You must show harmony with sky, earth, and water. The same harmony a protector must hold." Noah's chest tightened. He didn't feel like a protector yet... but the word echoed inside him. Kirra's father continued, "Bring me three sacred items. Not taken by force — found by spirit and guided by Country."

He raised a finger.

"One: An eagle feather. A symbol of protection, carried by the skies."

A second finger.

"Two: A Heart Gem. Pulled from the earth. Strong, unbroken. A bond that does not fade."

A third finger.

"And three: A Stone of Tides. Found where sea meets land. A symbol of balance. Courage that endures."

Noah absorbed every word. Kirra pressed her hand over her heart, eyes shimmering. "Dad... he can do this." Her father nodded slowly. "Perhaps. But the land must agree." Steve's feathers puffed with excitement. "A quest! Finally!"

Noah drew a steadying breath.

He would do it — not for glory.

For Kirra.

Noah stared at the carved stick between them, the firelight catching every groove and marking. It wasn't just wood — it was responsibility. A promise. A doorway to something larger than himself.

He inhaled deeply, steadied his shaking hands, and touched the stick with his fingertips.

"I accept," he said quietly. "I'll bring all three."

Kirra's breath caught, pride softening her features. Her hand settled on Noah's shoulder, grounding him. "You don't have to do this alone," she whispered.

Noah managed a small smile. "I know. But I want to prove I can stand on my own feet too."

Kirra's father watched them both, unreadable for a long moment. Then he nodded once — an approval rare and meaningful. "Return with those items, and you will have my blessing."

In the shadows, an elder murmured, "The boy walks a path meant for him."

Steve puffed out his chest. "Well! Obviously I'll supervise."

Frankie slipped off his branch and landed headfirst in the sand. "I'll... help too," he mumbled, dizzy.

Despite the nerves twisting inside him, Noah laughed softly.

The quest had begun.
 And something inside him — something old, something powerful — stirred at the edges of his spirit.

Noah woke before the birds did.

The camp was silent except for the soft hiss of dying coals. Noah crouched beside a small ember bed, tying the last knot on his carrying strap. He had packed lightly—water skin, a wrapped piece of damper, a woven pouch for whatever the land revealed to him. Nothing more. The sky was a pale grey, dawn stretching slowly across the treetops.

"You're really going before sunrise?" Kirra's voice came softly behind him.

Noah turned. She stood wrapped in a thin cloak, hair loose, eyes full of worry hidden beneath pride.

"I need to," he said. "Your father asked for spirit, not strength. And spirit listens best before the day wakes."

Kirra stepped closer, giving him a small woven charm. "For safety," she whispered. "My mum made it for me when I was little." Noah held it as if it were something sacred. "Thank you."

Steve clomped up beside them. "We are READY for adventure. I brought snacks."
Frankie staggered behind him carrying a giant leaf full of random objects. "I brought… everything!"

Kirra laughed softly. "You're not alone, Noah."

He looked at her — really looked — and nodded.

"No. I'm not."

And as the first sunlight touched the land, they set out.

The bush was different at sunrise — alive in a way that felt older than memory. Golden light broke through the treetops, painting shifting patterns on the ground as Noah led the way along a narrow track.

Steve paced beside him with a seriousness normally reserved for pretending to be wise. "Now, Noah," he said, lifting his chin dramatically, "the first rule of quests—"

"Don't listen to Steve," Frankie interrupted, tumbling over a fallen branch and popping up proudly.

"That is NOT the rule!" Steve snapped, feathers fluffing.

Wally trundled behind them, carrying a giant bundle of sticks, leaves, and at least one random stone. "I brought supplies," he said, slightly out of breath.

Noah glanced back and smiled. "Wally... that's just half a tree."

"It's useful!" the wombat insisted before tripping over a root.

Despite the humour, Noah felt something else thrumming beneath the laughter — a soft pull in his chest, like the land was guiding his steps.

Kirra's father had said the items must be found by spirit. And Noah could feel that spirit now... in the wind, in the earth under his feet, in the distant cry of a bird high above them.

The quest had begun in earnest.

And the land was watching.

They had barely walked another hundred steps when the wind shifted—soft, warm, carrying a distant cry from above. Noah stopped. Something tugged inside his chest, the same quiet pull he'd felt since dawn. Steve tilted his head. "Why are we stopping? Did someone forget snacks? Was it Frankie?"

Before Noah could answer, a shadow swept across the ground. All four of them looked up. High above the trees, wings wide as a spirit's embrace, a wedge-tailed eagle circled slow and deliberate. Sunlight caught the tips of its feathers, framing it in a golden shimmer.

Frankie gasped. "It's HUGE. It could eat me. Steve, protect me!"

Steve puffed up. "Nobody wants to eat you, Frankie."

Wally pointed toward the opposite direction. "I see it! ...Wait. No, that's a leaf." Noah didn't hear them. He felt the world narrow to the shape in the sky — powerful, steady, guiding. Kirra's father had spoken of spirit signs. Djama had spoken of fire in the blood. And here was the first sign of the quest:

The eagle.

Noah whispered, barely breathing, "Show me where to go."

As if it understood, the eagle banked sharply and flew toward the distant cliffs.

Steve straightened. "Well... that seems clear."

The quest had chosen its direction.

The path toward the cliffs grew steeper with every step, the soft bush track giving way to rough stone and loose gravel. Noah wiped sweat from his brow but pressed forward, eyes locked on the distant ledge where the eagle had come to rest.

"Who in the world invented rocks?" Wally groaned, slipping for the third time. "I'd like a word with them."

"Just lift your feet!" Frankie shouted from above, somehow leaping between stones like he weighed nothing at all.

Steve flapped his wings dramatically as he struggled upward. "This terrain is clearly designed for birds. But not me birds. More... flying birds."

Noah offered Wally a hand, pulling him up the next rise. "Careful. We're close."

The air grew quieter. Still. Heavy, in a peaceful way. As if the land itself waited.

When they reached a flat shelf halfway up the cliff, Noah froze.

The eagle stood above them on a stone outcrop — tall, majestic, watching them with an intelligence that made Noah's chest tighten. It did not fly away. It did not fear them. It simply... waited.

A warm breeze swept past Noah's face.

Steve whispered, reverent for once, "This is it. The sky's gift."

Noah stepped forward, heart pounding.

The first sacred item was near.

Noah climbed the final stretch alone. The wind whispered along the cliffside, brushing through his dreads and carrying the cry of distant birds. When he stepped onto the flat stone ledge, the eagle did not move — only turned its great head to meet his gaze. For a moment, Noah forgot to breathe. The bird's eyes were deep gold, ancient in a way he couldn't describe. It felt like looking into a memory older than people, older than story. Noah bowed his head instinctively, not because he should — but because it felt right.

"I'm here," he whispered. "If the land allows it... I ask for a feather. For protection."

The eagle unfolded its wings slightly, wind rippling across the ledge. A single loose feather lifted from its shoulder, caught in the breeze, and drifted downward — slow, deliberate, as if guided.

Noah reached out.

The feather landed gently in his hand.

Below, Steve gasped loudly. "HE DID IT! HE DID THE SKY THING!"

Frankie jumped up and down, nearly falling off the rock. Wally sniffled loudly, emotional for reasons even he didn't understand.

Noah held the feather to his chest.

The first sacred item was his.

The sky had accepted him.

The walk down the cliffs felt lighter than the climb up. Noah held the eagle feather close, feeling its softness against his palm — a reminder of the moment the sky had answered him. Every step carried new purpose. New weight. New hope. Steve marched proudly at his side, chest puffed out. "I always knew you were chosen material," he declared. "I mean... after me, obviously."Frankie swung a stick above his head.

"ONWARD! TO ITEM NUMBER TWO!"

Wally lumbered behind them with a sigh. "Does item number two involve... less climbing?" Noah smiled, but something tugged at him — the faint prickling sensation he'd felt the night before on the beach. He paused, staring out toward the forest below.A thin ribbon of pale mist drifted through the trees.

Not thick. Not close. But there. Watching.Waiting.

Steve followed his gaze, feathers tightening. "Noah...?"

Noah swallowed. "We keep moving. The land's with us. But so is something else."

They continued downward as the sun dipped behind the hills, painting the world in firelight and shadow.

Noah touched the feather again.

One gift found.
 Two more to earn.
 And the shadows that walked wrong were stirring.

CHAPTER 8 —
THE STONE OF TIDES

Dawn had not fully broken when Noah woke.

The camp still murmured in low sleep sounds — soft snores, crackling coals, the distant rhythm of waves.

Noah sat just beyond the shelters, tightening the strap of his carry bag. Inside, wrapped carefully in woven fibre, lay the eagle feather. The first gift.

He touched it briefly, feeling that same quiet power from the cliffside. Sky — done. Now the sea.

He glanced back toward the camp.

Kirra slept near her family's shelter, cloaked and peaceful, though a small crease still marked her brow even in rest.

Beyond her, Djama sat cross-legged in the half-light, eyes already open, watching Noah without surprise.

"The second path calls," the Elder said softly.

Noah nodded. "Stone of Tides."

Djama inclined his head. "The sea remembers fear... and courage. Go with both."

Steve clomped up beside them, feathers ruffled. "I had a vision we were leaving without me. It was horrible."

Frankie scrambled over a log, already chattering. Wally lumbered behind, blinking sleep from his eyes.

Noah rose, the weight of the feather and Kirra's charm grounding him.

Two elements down. One still to earn. And the sea waiting.

The path to the coast felt shorter this time — not because the distance had changed, but because Noah knew exactly where he was going. And what waited there.

Trees thinned with every step, giving way to low scrub and tougher grasses. The smell of salt grew stronger, mixing with the faint scent of char still clinging to Noah's memory from Big Red's fire.

Frankie bounced ahead, tail flicking. "So! What does a Stone of Tides look like? Big? Shiny? Glows in the dark? Talks?"

Wally puffed. "I hope it's soft. Rocks should really be softer."

Steve walked closer than usual, eyes scanning the path. "Stones shaped by time, waves, and patience. Unlike Frankie."

"Rude," Frankie muttered.

Noah barely heard them. In his mind, the beach replayed: Kirra's fingers digging into the sand; the way her voice shook when she saw the red coat; that pale face turned toward them through the mist.

The world had felt wrong that night.

Now he was walking willingly back into that wrongness. He exhaled slowly. "I'm not the same as I was then," he told himself.

Ahead, the whisper of waves grew louder, like breathing.

The sea was waiting.

They crested the last dune and the beach opened before them — wide, quiet, almost gentle in the early light. Almost. Noah stopped.

There it was: the curve of shoreline, the scattered driftwood, the place where their small fire had once glowed. And further down… the stretch of sand where the mist had parted like a curtain, revealing red.

His hands curled into fists before he realised.

"Same spot?" Steve asked softly.

"Yeah," Noah replied, voice low.

Frankie frowned. "Looks normal to me." Wally sniffed. "Smells like seaweed and regret."

Mist drifted above the water, thin and low, more like a sigh than a wall. No shapes. No coats. No hollow eyes.

But the feeling lingered — that sense of being watched by something that didn't belong.

Noah stepped down onto the sand. The grains were cold under his bare feet, damp from the tide. He forced his breathing to slow.

"I came here for a stone," he said quietly, more to the sea than to his friends. "Not for shadows."

The waves rolled in and out, calm and rhythmic, as if acknowledging his words.

He moved forward.

This time, he wouldn't run.

They fanned out along the rocky curve of the shoreline, where the ocean had carved pockets and pools into the stone. Noah moved slowly, letting his fingers trail through the water. Smooth pebbles, broken shells, shards of glinting rock — all ordinary, all wrong.

The Stone of Tides wouldn't just be pretty. It had to feel... right.

Frankie stuck his face into a pool and blew bubbles.

"THIS ONE'S NICE. I CLAIM IT AS FRANKIE ROCK."

"That's just a snail, mate," Steve said.

Wally stepped onto a slick patch of seaweed and immediately slid sideways, landing with a wet thump. "The ocean is a menace," he groaned.

Despite everything, Noah smiled faintly. He straightened, closed his eyes, and let Djama's words echo through him:

"The land speaks when the heart is quiet."

So he quieted.

The sound of waves folded around him. The push and pull, the soft crash, the retreat. The gull cries faded. Even Frankie's muttering dropped away. In the hush, Noah sensed something else — a gentle, steady pulse beneath the water. Not loud. Not dramatic. Just... constant.

He opened his eyes and followed it.

To a small tide pool glowing softly with reflected light.

The tide pool was small, cradled between two dark rocks like a held breath. Light struck the surface just right, turning it into a shallow mirror.

But Noah wasn't looking at the sky — he was looking beneath it.

There, resting between two larger stones, lay a smooth, rounded rock. Not bright. Not flashy. Just... balanced. Its surface was worn by time, veined faintly, colours deep and shifting like the sea at dusk.

He reached his hand toward the water, then stopped.

"Ask," Steve murmured quietly behind him.

Noah swallowed and whispered, "If the sea allows... I ask for this stone. To walk with courage.

To stay steady. For Kirra.

For our mob." The wave rolled in, spilling gently over the edge of the pool — cool water swirling around his wrist, then sliding back.

The stone shifted. Not with the tide. With intention.

It loosened from its resting place and rolled softly into Noah's waiting palm.

A shiver ran through him — not of cold, but of recognition.

Frankie gasped. "It moved. It actually moved."

Wally sniffled again. "Rocks... shouldn't make me emotional." Noah closed his fingers around the Stone of Tides.

The water had answered.

The moment Noah closed his hand around the Stone, the air changed.

The waves went quiet. Not softer — silent. No gull cries. No wind. The world seemed to hold its breath.

"Noah..." Steve whispered. "Look up. Slowly."

Noah lifted his gaze toward the surf. The mist at the water's edge was no longer drifting. It had drawn together, thick and heavy, shaping itself into a curved opening — an echo of the archway from that night.

Within it stood a tall figure in a long, tattered red coat. Knee-deep in the water. Unmoving.

Watching.

Its face was the same blank white mask of wrongness as before. Features blurred. Eyes like empty pits of moonlight. Frankie's frill snapped open with a scared rustle.

"Nope. Nope, I hate this. I hate all of this." Wally pressed himself against the rock, trembling.

Steve moved without thinking. He stepped in front of Noah, wings slightly lifted, body a barrier between boy and spirit. For a heartbeat, the air around him shimmered — as if something older, vaster, pushed at the edges of his form.

The figure tilted its head in that broken, unnatural way. The mist thickened. Then, as quickly as it had formed, the archway collapsed, swallowing the red coat with it.

The waves returned. But the message was clear.

They had been seen.

They didn't speak for a long time. The beach behind them looked ordinary again — waves breaking in soft white lines, mist thinning into harmless ribbons. But the memory of that blank white face clung to Noah like cold water.

He rubbed his thumb along the Stone of Tides, feeling the grooves and curves worn by time. It felt solid. Real. A promise of steadiness.

"Okay," Frankie said loudly, because silence made him worse. "So! Great news: you have your stone. Less great news: the walking mistake in the red coat definitely knows your face now."

"Frankie," Steve warned.

"I'm just saying!"

Wally shuffled closer to Noah. "I liked it better when the scariest thing around here was Steve's snoring."

Steve huffed. "My snoring is majestic."

Despite himself, Noah smiled weakly. He glanced back one last time. Nothing stood at the shoreline now — but the sea felt full of eyes. He turned away.

"I'm not running from it," he said quietly.

Steve nodded, voice lower than usual. "You don't have to. Just don't face it alone." Noah tightened his grip on the stone.

Feather for the sky. Stone for the sea.

Only the earth remained.

The further they walked from the shore, the louder the world became again. Birdsong returned first, then the rustle of leaves, the chatter of small creatures waking to the day.

The normal sounds of Country did what they always did — soothed, reminded, steadied. Frankie, however, did the opposite.

"And THEN," he proclaimed, waving his arms, "the mist did a weird twisty thing, and the coat guy was like 'ooooo I'm spooky,' and Steve went all glowing hero—"

"I did not glow," Steve said quickly.

"You totally glowed," Wally whispered, impressed.

Noah walked ahead, listening but not interrupting.

The Stone pressed warm and solid against his side, its weight a steady reminder of why he'd come. Not just for a quest.
Not just for Kirra's father's approval.

For Kirra. For Big Red and Little Red. For all of them.

The mob.

As the scent of smoke grew stronger, the outline of camp came into view between the trees — shelters, fires, figures beginning their morning routines. Noah took a deep breath.

Two trials complete.

His chest still ached with the image of the red coat in the waves — but beneath that fear, something else was growing.

Resolve.

Kirra's father waited near their shelter, as if he had known exactly when Noah would return. Noah slowed as he approached, dust and sea-salt clinging to his skin, clothes damp at the edges.

Steve, Frankie, and Wally stopped a respectful distance behind him.

Kirra stood beside her father, hands clasped in front of her. Her eyes went straight to Noah's face, searching, then dropped to the small pouch at his side.

Noah untied it carefully.

He cupped the Stone of Tides in both hands and held it out. The morning light picked up its subtle colours — deep greys, blues, greens, like storms waiting beyond the horizon.

"This," Noah said, voice steady, "was given by the sea. Not taken. It... moved on its own. Like it chose to come."

Kirra's father studied the stone for a long moment before taking it.

His thumb traced the surface, feeling the grooves shaped by time. His eyes, when they lifted, were softer than before.

"Sky has seen you," he said. "Now the tides have as well."

Kirra let out a breath she'd been holding. Behind them, Frankie whispered, "Two down. One very scary earth rock to go."

Wally nodded solemnly. "I believe in him."

So did Kirra's father now — even if he didn't say it aloud.

Later, when the camp had settled into its morning rhythm, Djama found Noah standing at the edge of the clearing, watching Kirra and her father.

They were wrapping the eagle feather and the Stone of Tides together in a small woven bundle — sky and sea, held in the same embrace.

"You have done well," Djama said, stepping up beside him.

Noah shrugged lightly, though pride warmed his cheeks.

"The land helped. The sea did too. And the spirit walker... watched." Djama's eyes darkened.

"Yes. The ones who walk wrong do not like to be ignored." "Why show up when I took the stone?" Noah asked quietly. "Was it a warning?"

"Maybe," Djama replied. "Or maybe it was afraid."

Noah blinked. "Afraid? Of what?" Djama's gaze rested on him with a small, knowing smile. "Of what you will become." A breeze stirred.

For just a heartbeat, the air around Noah felt charged — like the moment before a storm, when lightning is still deciding where to strike. Djama's hand settled on his shoulder. "Sky and sea have answered you. Only earth remains." Noah looked toward the distant hills.

"The Heart Gem," he said.

Djama nodded.

"And after that, Noah... the Marra'kai Ceremony."

The path was clear now. And Noah stepped forward to meet it.

CHAPTER 9 – THE HEART (GEM)

Noah didn't realise how tightly he'd been holding himself until he saw Big Red standing at the edge of camp.

The kangaroo looked different now — still a little thinner, still carrying a quiet sadness in his eyes, but stronger. Steadier. Little Red pressed against his side like a shadow, ears flicking at every sound.

Big Red's gaze dropped to the pouch at Noah's hip, then lifted back to his face.

"Heard you've got one more thing to find," he said, voice rough but firm. He thumped his tail once, sending a puff of dust into the air. "And that you'll need a proper digger."

Little Red tried to copy him, tail flicking awkwardly. The tiny thump barely disturbed a leaf.

Noah laughed — a real laugh this time, not the brittle kind that came after fear. "Yeah," he said. "Heart Gem. From the earth."

Frankie puffed his chest. "I'm excellent at digging. I once buried Wally's lunch and even I couldn't find it again."

"That's... not helping," Wally murmured, clutching a new snack protectively.

From across the camp, Noah caught sight of Djama and Kirra's father, standing over the small woven bundle that held the feather and the Stone of Tides.

Two trials complete.

One left.

And he wouldn't be facing it alone.

Noah didn't realise how tightly he'd been holding himself until he saw Big Red standing at the edge of camp.

The kangaroo looked different now — still a little thinner, still carrying a quiet sadness in his eyes, but stronger. Steadier.

Little Red pressed against his side like a shadow, ears flicking at every sound.

Big Red's gaze dropped to the pouch at Noah's hip, then lifted back to his face.

"Heard you've got one more thing to find," he said, voice rough but firm. He thumped his tail once, sending a puff of dust into the air. "And that you'll need a proper digger."

Little Red tried to copy him, tail flicking awkwardly. The tiny thump barely disturbed a leaf. Noah laughed — a real laugh this time, not the brittle kind that came after fear. "Yeah," he said. "Heart Gem. From the earth."

Frankie puffed his chest. "I'm excellent at digging. I once buried Wally's lunch and even I couldn't find it again."

"That's... not helping," Wally murmured, clutching a new snack protectively.

From across the camp, Noah caught sight of Djama and Kirra's father, standing over the small woven bundle that held the feather and the Stone of Tides.

Two trials complete.

One left.

And he wouldn't be facing it alone.

Noah didn't expect half the camp to watch them leave, but when he reached the edge of the clearing, people had quietly gathered—some pretending to do chores, others openly staring with small, proud smiles.

Big Red thumped his tail once. "Right then. Earth stuff. Digging. Strong point of mine." Little Red mimicked the thump with a tiny squeak.

Steve strutted ahead. "As official guide of this expedition, I propose—"

Frankie cut him off. "You are not the guide. I am the danger detector."

Wally raised a paw. "I brought snacks."

Noah laughed, warm and real. It felt good.

Before stepping into the bush, he glanced back one last time. Kirra stood beside Djama, hands clasped, eyes full of worry and something softer. Djama gave a slow nod—approval, belief, and warning all in one. Noah touched the side of his pouch where the other two gifts rested with Kirra's father.

Sky.
Sea.
Now earth.

As they moved beneath the gum canopy, sunlight scattered across the path like broken gold. Birds called overhead. The land felt alive in a new way—listening, waiting. Big Red leaned close and whispered, "We'll find it, kid. Country doesn't hide what's meant to be found."

And Noah believed him.

The creek bed was nothing like the sea or sky. It was quiet. Still. Heavy.

Noah crouched beside the dry channel and let the dirt sift through his fingers.

The ground here felt older—like it held memories deeper than anything spoken aloud. But it didn't speak quickly. It didn't rush. And that tested him far more than cliffs or crashing waves ever had.

Big Red sniffed the air, then scratched thoughtfully at the cracked earth. "There's something here... hiding under us. Country's shifting."

Frankie wedged himself into a narrow space between two rocks.

"Stand back! My danger-sensing frill will alert us to any—OUCH." He immediately hit his head.

Steve sighed loudly from atop a boulder. "Try doing it with dignity for once."

Wally, halfway across the creek bed, had already dug an enthusiastic hole.

"Found something!" They all hurried over. It was a stick.
Wally looked crushed. "Still useful..." Noah managed a smile, but frustration prickled at him.

He closed his eyes and steadied his breath.

The land wouldn't respond to impatience.

He pressed his palm flat against the ground, feeling its warmth, its weight, its silence.

Somewhere beneath the surface... something waited.

He could feel it, faint but real. The earth was listening. And beginning to stir.

Time passed differently on the earth's path. On the cliffs, Noah had felt wind and height lift him. At the sea, the waves had spoken.

But here... everything was still. Too still. Like the land wanted him to sit with himself before offering anything more.

Noah dragged his fingers through the dry soil again. Nothing. Just dust and stubborn silence.

Frankie collapsed dramatically beside him. "We're going to grow old out here. I'll be a fossil. A very handsome fossil."

Steve ignored him and stepped closer, resting one warm wing against Noah's shoulder. "The land doesn't rush, mate," he said gently.

"Neither should you." Big Red nodded, ears drooping slightly.

"Heart things take time. You of all people know that."

Noah exhaled slowly. He did know. Everything he'd faced — Kirra's fear, the fire, the spirit walker in the waves — had taught him that strength wasn't loud. It wasn't fast. It was steady. He closed his eyes, letting frustration fall away.

Kirra's face came to him. Her voice. Her trust. Then Wally's laughter. Big Red's grief turning to hope. Steve's endless loyalty.

His mob. Noah pressed his palm to the ground again — not demanding this time, just present. And beneath his hand...

He felt it. Not a sound, not a movement — a hum.

A heartbeat.

The earth answering.

The hum grew stronger beneath Noah's hand — gentle at first, like a memory waking. Then the ground trembled. Not enough to frighten. Just enough to answer.

Big Red stepped back, eyes widening. "Noah... the ground's moving." Steve's feathers shot upright. "Nobody panic! Except maybe panic a little!"

Wally gasped and pointed. "LOOK! THE DIRT IS GLOWING!" A thin crack split the earth in front of Noah's palm. Light seeped through — faint, blue, pulsing slowly like a heartbeat.

The heartbeat of Country. Frankie scrambled onto Wally's head for height, frill rattling with excitement. "He's doing EARTH MAGIC! Noah is doing EARTH MAGIC!"

Noah didn't move. He couldn't. Something inside him — something old, something calling — rose to meet the tremor beneath his hand.

A warmth spread across his skin.
Soft lines of light flickered along his arm, the same markings that had glowed during the fire... and again at the sea.

He stared at them in awe.

Big Red whispered, "Djama said your spirit was waking... mate, it's waking right now."

The light in the cracks brightened.

The earth shifted, revealing the dark mouth of a small opening.

And inside it...
a deeper, steadier glow waited.

Noah lowered his hand into the glowing crack.
The soil was warm — warmer than sunlight, warmer than fire — as if the earth itself exhaled against his skin. His fingers brushed something smooth. Round. Solid. Alive.

The ground pulsed once more, a gentle thump that travelled up his arm and into his chest.

Then the soil loosened around the object, lifting it toward his hand as though offering it.

Noah drew it out carefully. The Heart Gem rested in his palm — a stone no bigger than an egg, glowing softly from within.

Its centre shimmered deep red, surrounded by swirling bands of blue like flowing rivers. The surface felt warm, beating faintly... like it carried the heart of Country itself.

Big Red stepped closer, voice trembling. "That's it... that's the one."

Frankie shoved his face beside Noah's hand. "I SAW IT FIRST—okay no I didn't but STILL—LOOK AT IT!"

Wally hugged Noah tightly, nearly knocking him over. "You did it! You really did it!"

Steve swallowed hard, brushing a wing across his face. "It's just dust," he muttered, fooling no one.

Noah held the Heart Gem to his chest.

"For Kirra," he whispered.
"For my mob."
"For who I'm becoming."

The earth had accepted him.

He was nearly ready for the ceremony.

The walk back felt different — lighter somehow, yet heavier with meaning.
Noah held the Heart Gem close, its warmth spreading through his fingers and up his arm, settling deep in his chest. His spirit-markings flickered faintly, almost shyly, as if waking for the first time.

Big Red walked beside him with a pride that softened the ache still living in his eyes. Little Red hopped close behind, comforted by the group's steady presence.

Behind them, Frankie launched into the twentieth retelling of the moment.

"And THEN the ground literally opened and Noah reached in like—WHOOSH—and the rock was like—SPARKLE SPARKLE—"

Wally nodded seriously. "I felt the sparkle. In my toes."

Steve walked on the other side of Noah, quieter than usual. "The land's with you, kid," he said softly. "All of it. Even the parts that don't glow."

Ahead, the bush began to thicken again. Birds circled above, their shadows sweeping across the path — one of them briefly shaped like the eagle that had granted Noah his first gift.

Kangaroos paused in the distance, heads turning in his direction.

Noah felt it:

The land wasn't just watching him.

It was recognising him.

And guiding him home.

By the time they reached the heart of the camp, word had already spread.
Families stepped quietly out of their shelters, forming a widening circle around Noah and his friends.

The cleansing fires burned low, glowing beneath curls of pale smoke.

Children hushed each other, sensing something important.

Djama stood at the center, staff planted firmly in the earth.

Kirra and her father waited beside him.

Noah stepped forward. His hands didn't shake this time. He untied the small pouch across his chest and withdrew the three sacred items — the Eagle Feather, the Stone of Tides, and the Heart Gem. Each one seemed to catch the morning light differently: sky, sea, and earth, held together in one moment.

He bowed his head and offered them to Djama.

"For my mob," he said quietly. "For Kirra. And for the ceremony."

Djama accepted the items with both hands, eyes brightened by something deeper than pride — recognition.

"Your trials are complete," the Elder said, voice echoing across the clearing. "Sky has seen you. Tides have answered you. Earth has welcomed you."

Kirra's father placed a hand on Noah's shoulder. Kirra's eyes shimmered.

Around them, the mob erupted in a rising cheer. Noah breathed in. He was ready.

The Marra'kai Ceremony awaited.

Night settled over the camp like a warm cloak.

Torches flickered one by one, forming a glowing ring around the ceremonial grounds. Families gathered in respectful silence, faces lit by amber firelight. Even the wind seemed to pause, waiting with them.

Noah stood at the edge of the fire circle, the woven bundle pressed gently to his chest. Inside it, the Eagle Feather, the Stone of Tides, and the Heart Gem rested together for the first time — sky, sea, and earth united.

Djama knelt by the ceremonial fire, crushing ochres into fine powder. The glow of the flames reflected in his deep-set eyes as he stirred the pigments slowly, reverently.

"You've walked the paths," Djama said as Noah approached. "Now you stand at the place where all paths meet."

Noah swallowed, heart thudding.

He felt the mob behind him — their trust, their pride, their hope.
He felt Kirra's gaze as she stepped forward, hands clasped in anticipation.

He felt her father watching, not with judgment, but with belief.

Djama placed a hand over the bundle.

"When the fire rises," he whispered, "the boy you were will fall away. And the man chosen by spirit will stand."

The flames swayed — as if answering.

The Marra'kai Ceremony was about to begin.

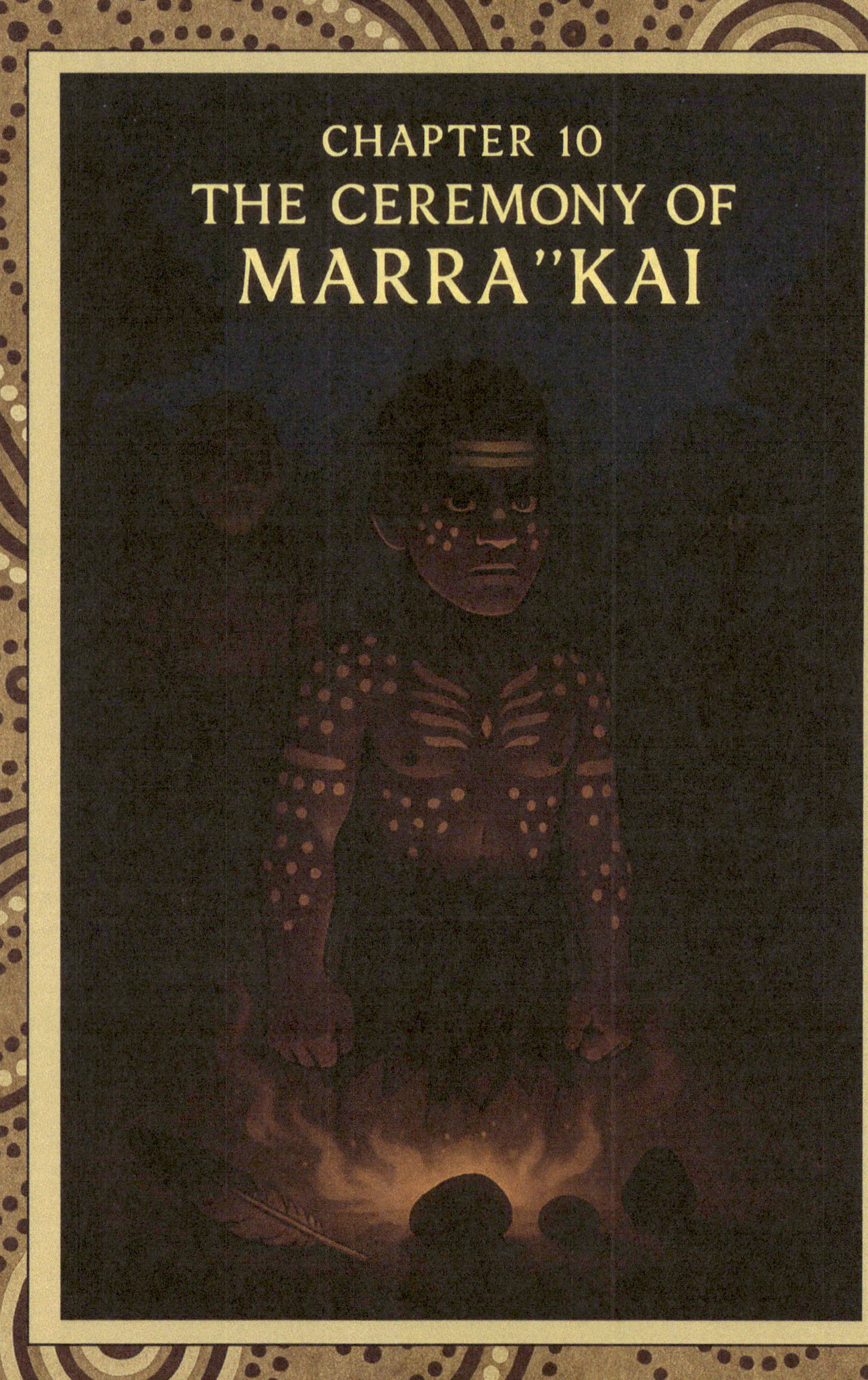

CHAPTER 10
THE CEREMONY OF
MARRA"KAI

Night rose around the camp like a slow tide.

By the time the last light drained from the horizon, torches had been planted in a wide circle beyond the shelters.

Flames licked upward, painting the trunks of the gum trees in shifting gold. People moved quietly toward the clearing, feet soft on the earth, voices lowered in respect.

Noah stood at the edge of the circle, clutching a woven bundle against his chest.

Inside it, wrapped in fibre and leaves, lay the eagle feather, the Stone of Tides, and the Heart Gem. Sky. Sea. Earth.

All the paths he had walked, all the fear and courage and laughter and hurt, now resting in his hands.

His stomach fluttered like a trapped bird.

Djama waited within the circle, staff planted in the centre beside a low fire.

Small bowls of ochre and white clay sat at his feet, their surfaces glowing softly.

Elders took their places around him, faces lined with years of story.

Kirra slipped in beside her family, eyes already searching for Noah. Big Red and Little Red settled near the back, both strangely quiet. Steve stood just outside the circle, feathers slicked down for once, gaze fixed on Noah with a seriousness that didn't match his usual chaos.

Djama lifted his staff.

"The Marra'kai begins," he said, voice rolling through the clearing like distant thunder. "Tonight, boy... you step from who you were into who you are meant to be."

Djama knelt before him with the same patient care he might give a newborn child.

In the coolamon beside him, four colours waited: yellow ochre, white clay, burnt charcoal, and red earth. The same colours, Djama had said, that touched Marrakai's skin when the world was younger and wilder.

"Life," he murmured, dipping his fingers into the ochre and pressing the first dots along Noah's chest. "Spirit." A swipe of white followed, tracing gentle arcs over his shoulders.

"Strength." Charcoal smudged in small clusters where muscle met bone.

"And Country." Red earth warmed beneath Djama's touch as he circled Noah's sternum with careful marks, a path for something greater to travel.

Noah held still, eyes lowered, feeling each touch like a small spark. The paint was cool at first, then strangely warm, as if it carried memories from every boy who had ever sat here before him.

He glanced up once.

Kirra watched from the edge of the circle, hands knotted together, pride and worry warring in her eyes.

Behind her, Steve stood like a carved totem, feathers flat, gaze unreadable.

Djama's fingers moved to Noah's back, sketching the beginnings of wings.

"The body remembers," the Elder whispered. "Now we see what the spirit remembers too."

Djama lifted his staff, and the entire clearing seemed to inhale.

When he spoke, it wasn't loud — but it was old. A sound shaped by stone, by fire, by the first guardians who walked this Country.

The Marra'kai Chant.

Low and steady at first, rising like wind pushing through a canyon.

The other elders joined him one by one, their voices weaving into his: deep, layered, resonant.

The air vibrated. The fire shifted, its flames stretching higher as if called by the sound.

Noah felt the chant in his bones. Each note seemed to travel through the paint on his skin — along the dot clusters, down the lines over his chest, across the wings marked on his back. His breath shortened. His heartbeat synced to the rhythm.

Kirra pressed her hand over her mouth, tears gathering. Big Red leaned so far forward he nearly toppled. Frankie clung to Wally's fur, eyes round.

But Steve... Steve stood perfectly still. His feathers lay flat against his body, eyes shining with something ancient, something mournful. He mouthed the words silently — because he had sung them before.

Long ago.

The chant rose, brightening the fire, thickening the air.

The spirits were listening.

The chant ended like a door closing. All sound vanished — not faded, but vanished. No wind.
 No crackle of fire. No shifting feet or whisper of leaves.

Just stillness. Djama moved with deliberate care, lowering himself until he knelt directly before Noah. His palms pressed against Noah's chest, right over the ochre lines that traced spirit channels across his skin.

"Noah," Djama whispered, his voice carrying through the silence like a drop in a vast pool,
 "let the spirits judge.
 Let Spirit Blood rise...
 if it lives in you."

Noah swallowed.

 His whole body felt warm — not from the fire, but from something beneath his skin, something waking.

The elders placed their palms flat on the earth.

Kirra leaned forward, breath trembling. Big Red leaned too far forward and tipped sideways with a soft thud. Frankie slapped a hand over his mouth to keep from yelling

. Djama closed his eyes... and the earth hummed.

Not enough to shake the ground — just enough for Noah to feel the vibration through his bones.
 A faint glow pulsed beneath the paint on his chest. Kirra gasped.

Steve's feathers lifted, sensing what was coming.

The spirits were answering.

Noah blinked. And the world tore open.

The ceremony circle dissolved into a wash of gold and shadow, as though the firelight had stretched itself thin and become a doorway.

Embers floated around him, frozen like tiny suns. The ground beneath him pulsed with warm light, forming glowing veins that spread out across the land like living pathways.

A rush of wind — but he felt it only in his spirit, not his skin.

Then he saw it.

A colossal Eagle Spirit descended from a sky made of swirling ochre and smoke. Its wings stretched far beyond anything real, shimmering with patterns older than story. Its eyes burned bright, seeing straight through him. Behind it, rising from the golden earth, stood a towering emu-shaped silhouette.

Marrakai.

Not the bumbling Steve Noah knew — but the ancient guardian he once was. Its shape loomed like a mountain, protective and unyielding.

Noah's breath caught as the vision swelled. Mist rolled in on the edges — and within it flickered pale figures. Red coats. Hollow eyes. Spirit walkers watching him from the horizon of his own vision.

A voice — not loud, but heavy with truth — whispered through the wind:

"When the land trembles… the Eagle Spirit must rise."

Noah gasped and snapped back into the circle, chest heaving. The vision wasn't imagined.

It was a calling.

Noah crashed back into himself with a sharp inhale, the vision dissolving like smoke in wind.

The ground steadied beneath him — but the world felt different now, too loud, too bright, too alive.

Djama stumbled backward. The Elder's eyes were wide, shining with something between terror and wonder.

"No…" he whispered, voice shaking. "It cannot be… after all these generations…"

Around the circle, elders rose to their feet. Some pressed hands to their mouths, others murmured prayers in old tongue. A few stepped forward, reaching toward Noah before stopping themselves — as though afraid the air around him might burn.

Kirra leaned forward, breath trembling. "Noah…?"

Steve stood rigid, feathers slicked tight, his throat bobbing. He looked at Noah with an expression Noah had never seen before — something ancient, like recognition.

The fire at the circle's center crackled violently, sending a stream of sparks swirling upward. Smoke twisted into shapes — wings, feathers, a rising eagle silhouette that faded as quickly as it formed.

Djama pressed a trembling hand to his chest.
"Noah… the spirits answered you. They answered you directly."

Noah swallowed, his heart thudding. "What does it mean?"

Djama's voice broke.

"It means… Spirit Blood has returned."

Djama lifted his staff, and the fire obeyed. Flames surged upward, stretching high into the night sky as if pulled by some invisible force. The wind circled Noah's feet, brushing dust into soft spirals. The elders fell into stunned silence. Then Djama spoke. His voice carried the weight of every generation before them — every elder, every protector, every story ever passed down around firelight.

"By the old laws…" Djama began.

The crowd leaned in. "By the spirits of sky, earth, and sea…"

The wind hissed softly in answer. "By Marrakai's own songline…"

Steve inhaled sharply, feathers trembling. Djama pointed the staff toward Noah.

"This boy carries the spark of the Eagle Spirit."

The camp erupted.

Cries of shock. Gasps. Cheers. Prayers. Children staring wide-eyed. Elders pressing hands to trembling hearts.

Wally burst into tears instantly. Frankie screamed, "I knew it!"

Big Red keeled backward in a dramatic faint while Little Red smacked his cheek to wake him. Noah could barely breathe. Kirra stepped forward, eyes glistening with pride and fear entwined. "Noah… you're—" He shook his head, overwhelmed, voice small. "I'm just me."

Djama's voice softened.

"Not anymore."

Above them, the fire cracked —
 and somewhere in the distance, a lone eagle cried.

The fire roared upward without wind. The smoke rose in a twisting column, swirling with purpose. Colour and heat rippled through the air as Djama stepped forward, planting his staff in the earth with a crack that echoed like thunder.

"Spirits of old!" Djama called, voice deep and trembling.
"Hear us! The boy stands ready!"

Noah felt the air tighten around him, wrapping him like a second skin. A warmth spread beneath his painted chest and along the patterns on his arms. It wasn't painful — just powerful, like waking muscles he never knew he had. Kirra pressed a hand to her mouth, eyes shimmering.
"Noah... your markings..."

Steve whispered, half reverent, half terrified, "He's doing it... he's actually doing it."
Djama's eyes reflected firelight as he looked down at Noah. "The prophecy speaks of this moment. When the land trembles... when shadows return... the Eagle Spirit stirs again."

Elders gasped softly, some taking a step back, others stepping closer with reverence.

Big Red muttered, "Oh no... he's glowing. Again."
Wally whimpered. Frankie fainted for dramatic effect.

The smoke above Noah shifted... widening... stretching...

It was unmistakable now.

A shape of wings.

Ancestors were watching.

And judging.

The fire cracked like a clap of thunder. Every head turned as the ceremony circle filled with light — not bright, not blinding, but pulsing. A soft glow throbbed beneath Noah's painted skin, pushing through the ochre and clay in a pattern older than memory.

A collective gasp rippled through the mob. Steve whispered, voice trembling, "It's starting... he's hearing them."

Kirra moved closer without thinking. Her hand brushed Noah's arm — and she felt it too. A warmth, steady and ancient, humming through him like a heartbeat shared with the land itself.

Noah staggered a step, breath catching. The world around him blurred for a moment, shapes bending like heat haze. He heard whispers — not voices, but impressions.

Wind. Wings. Fire. Earth. The echo of something calling his name.

Djama's voice boomed across the circle.
"Behold! The spirit marks awaken. The ancestors recognise him!"

Elders bowed their heads. Children clutched their parents. Wally sobbed openly.
Frankie shouted, "HE'S GLOWING AGAIN—EVERYBODY REMAIN CALM!" despite remaining the least calm of all.

But Noah wasn't scared this time.

He steadied himself, standing taller through the tremble in his legs.

The spirits weren't testing him anymore.

They were answering him.

The chants faded into memory, leaving only the crackle of dying torches and the soft hum of night insects. The mob drifted away in small groups, whispering about what they had witnessed — about the glow in Noah's skin, the shimmer in the smoke, the wings they swore they saw.

Noah stayed where he stood. His breath was slow. Deep. Heavy with everything he did not yet understand.

Djama stepped beside him, placing a steady hand on his painted shoulder.
"You walked well tonight, boy."

"It... it felt like something inside me was waking up," Noah whispered. "Like it already knew the chant."

Djama nodded. "Because it did. Spirit Blood remembers its path."

Noah swallowed hard. "Does this mean... I really could be—"

"Tomorrow," Djama said gently. "Tonight, you rest. The dawn will bring what it must."

Behind them, Kirra lingered at the circle's edge, her eyes warm, shining with pride and fear all at once. When Noah met her gaze, she mouthed silently:

I'm here.

Steve leaned against Noah's leg. "Don't worry, mate. If you explode into a giant eagle spirit, I'll talk you through it."

The ground trembled softly — distant, but real.

Djama's voice lowered.

"When you wake, Noah... you will not be the same."

BAAN MURRANG
CHAPTER 11
BAAN ASCENDING

Dawn had barely touched the horizon when Noah opened his eyes.

He hadn't truly slept — not with the echoes of the Marra'kai chant still humming beneath his skin, not with the warmth of the dot-art glowing faintly through the night.

Every time he closed his eyes, he saw wings. Felt wind. Heard the distant cry of something calling him forward.

He stepped quietly out of the shelter area, breath misting in the morning chill. The world felt... paused. Waiting. Djama found him at the edge of the clearing, as though guided there by instinct more ancient than words.

"You feel it," Djama said softly.

Noah nodded. "It's like everything inside me is... moving."

"The spirits do their work at dawn," Djama murmured. "Today... they finish what they began."

A soft rustle came beside them. Steve trotted out of the shadows, unusually serious, his golden eyes sharper than usual.

"No wandering off without your bodyguard," he muttered — but his voice carried weight, a tremble of knowing.

From the camp's edge, Kirra watched them, her hands clasped at her heart, hope and fear tangled on her face. Noah inhaled deeply. Whatever he was becoming — whatever waited for him —

starts now.

Noah hadn't walked more than fifty steps when the earth shivered beneath him.

A soft tremor — barely enough to shift the dust — but unmistakable.

Birds shot from the treetops in a frantic cloud, filling the sky with beating wings and startled cries.

The air seemed to tighten, pulling inward around him like a held breath. Steve froze mid-stride.

"There it is," he whispered.

"There what is?" Noah asked, though he already felt the answer swelling inside his chest.

"The land's warning," Steve murmured, eyes fixed on the horizon.

Djama stepped beside them, staff glowing a deep, steady amber. "The ground knows before we do. Always has." Noah swallowed, heart pounding as another faint tremor rippled through the soil. His ceremony markings responded — tiny sparks of gold flickering beneath the paint, pulsing with each heartbeat.

"What's happening to me?" Noah breathed.

Djama's voice was quiet, reverent. "Your spirit hears the call. When the land trembles... the protector must rise." Noah looked toward the distant hills — and his breath hitched.

Far to the north, barely visible through dawn haze, a thin column of black smoke curled into the sky. He didn't know what it meant yet. But Steve did.

And the land did.

And both were telling him:
Your time has come.

The clearing welcomed them like an ancient heartbeat. Noah stepped into its center—and the world changed. His foot touched the earth, and a sudden rush of warmth surged through his legs, up his spine, into his chest.

He gasped, stumbling forward as light burst beneath his skin.

The markings Djama had painted only hours before began to glow, gold pushing through ochre like dawn breaking through the horizon.

"Noah!" Kirra called from the edge of camp, but her voice felt distant, muffled by the roar building inside him. Djama lifted his staff. "It begins!" he cried, voice trembling. "Spirit Blood awakens!"

Noah dropped to one knee as the next pulse hit—stronger, deeper. The earth beneath his palms throbbed with power, vibrating like a drum stretched by the hands of the ancestors. The air whipped around him, lifting dust and leaves into a spiraling ring.

Steve stepped forward, wings half-spread, feathers crackling with faint gold. "Breathe, mate," he said softly. "Just breathe. You're not breaking. You're becoming."

Noah's chest markings flared, lines of fire racing across his ribs and shoulders. A cry tore from his throat—not pain, not fear—

Awakening.

The land had called.

And Noah was answering

The wind rose suddenly—not from any weather Noah had ever felt, but from something older, deeper.

It circled the clearing, twisting into a spiraling column that lifted leaves and dust into the air. And inside that swirling breath… shapes began to form.

Djama stepped back, eyes shining with tears. "The ancestors…" he whispered. "They gather for him."

Noah lifted his head as warmth ignited along his spine.

His back markings pulsed in perfect rhythm with the earth beneath him.

Gold spread across his shoulders like unfolding wings waiting to be born.

From the edge of the light, faint figures emerged—warriors with spears, elders draped in ceremonial ochres, spirit eagles that shimmered like constellations made flesh. They circled him, silent and watching. Noah felt them—not as strangers, but as memories carved into his bones.

A cry echoed above, deep and resonant. Noah looked toward Steve.

For a heartbeat, Steve's outline shattered—his emu shape dissolving into a towering eagle of blinding gold. Wings vast. Eyes ancient. Marrakai revealed. Then the shimmering folded back, leaving Steve panting and very much an emu again.

"Pretend you didn't see that," Steve muttered.

But Noah had seen.

And the ancestors had too.

Their wings, their voices, their power—were calling him forward.

Noah's breath caught as a new heat surged up his spine—hot, pulsing, alive.

The markings on his back burst into brilliant gold, flaring outward in long sweeping arcs.

Light spilled across the clearing, so bright the mob shielded their eyes.

Djama dropped to one knee.

"No... it can't be..." he whispered. "The Wings of Baan..."

Noah staggered forward as the light sharpened, the shapes on his skin lifting—first as shimmering outlines, then as feathers of pure energy forming in the air behind him.

They weren't physical, not yet. But they were real.

Power thrummed through Noah's bones, ancient and new all at once. He could feel the spirits moving with him—guiding, shaping, awakening.

A cry tore from his throat, not pain, not fear—something older, something that came from the marrow of the earth.

It echoed across the sky, answered by a deeper call from somewhere far above. Kirra pressed both hands to her mouth, tears streaking down her face.

"Noah..." Steve stepped closer, voice shaking.

"Easy, mate... let it happen. You were born for this." The wings of light stretched wider.

Longer. Brighter. The land trembled beneath him.

For the first time, Noah wasn't just standing on Country—
Country was rising through him.

The light that had roared from Noah's body softened—still bright, still burning, but now controlled. Guided.

A wind rose from nowhere, circling the clearing in a slow, reverent spiral. Leaves floated upward, suspended in the glow. The shadows bent, drawn toward Noah like iron to a magnet.

Then the air split with a deep, resonant call.

A shape materialised behind Noah—vast, majestic, ancient.

An Emu spirit so large its wings stretched from one end of the clearing to the other. Its feathers shimmered like starlit gold, each movement humming with power older than songlines.

Marrakai.

The First Protector.

The spirit leaned forward, its beak lowering until it hovered just above Noah's shoulder. A voice—felt more than heard—echoed inside Noah's mind: "I have watched you since first breath."

Noah's knees nearly gave out.
"Wh—why me?" he whispered.

"Because the land chose you.
Because your heart listens.
Because danger rises."

Steve stepped beside Noah, bowing his head deeply. For the first time, his outline warped —an eagle's form shimmering beneath his emu disguise. Noah stared at him, breath catching.
"Steve…?" Steve didn't meet his eyes.

"Surprise," he muttered softly.

The clearing exploded with wind. Not violent—powerful. Purposeful. A current that knew exactly where it wanted to go.

Noah felt the ground slip away beneath him, but he wasn't afraid.

The wings behind him—golden, ancient, alive—beat once, then again, lifting him upward. Leaves spiraled around him, scattering like sparks from a sacred fire.

Gasps rippled through the mob.

Djama dropped to one knee, tears streaking down his cheeks.
"An ascendant…" he whispered. "After all these generations… the Eagle Spirit walks again."

Kirra reached out toward him, her voice trembling with pride.
"Noah…"

He drifted higher, the markings on his skin glowing so intensely they seemed carved from light. Every breath felt fuller. Every heartbeat louder. Stronger. Connected to the land beneath and the sky above.

Below, Steve stood perfectly still—no jokes, no wobbling, no chaos. His feathers shimmered with a faint ancestral glow, the spirit of Marrakai flickering just beneath the surface. For a heartbeat, Noah hovered—weightless, endless. An eagle's cry tore through the dawn.

It came from him. The mob gasped, some falling backward in awe.

Noah's eyes widened. He wasn't dreaming.

He was becoming.

The protector had taken flight.

Noah's feet touched the earth as gently as a falling leaf. The wings behind him folded slow and deliberate, still glowing, still warm, still humming with ancient power.

His markings pulsed in soft waves, fading and brightening like living gold under his skin. Kirra reached him first, breath trembling.

"Noah... you flew."

He could only nod. He didn't have words yet. Not for this. Djama pressed a hand to Noah's forehead, voice cracking.

"The spirits have chosen. Marrakai has spoken. The Eagle Spirit rises once more."

The ground rumbled. Not the soft tremor from the ceremony's awakening—this was deeper. Angrier. The earth itself warning them. Small stones rattled. Dust lifted. Steve turned sharply north, feathers bristling. "...No."

Noah followed his gaze. In the far distance, beyond the hills and gum trees, a thin black pillar of smoke rose into the sky—too straight, too dark, too controlled to be natural.

And in the drifting mist along the treetops, Noah glimpsed something familiar:

A flicker of red.
A pale shape.
Watching.

The same wrongness from the shore. Kirra's hand tightened around his. Djama whispered, "The land trembles... because danger has landed."

Noah's wings glowed brighter.

The protector had awoken just in time.

One by one, the rest of the mob emerged from the shelters, drawn by the trembling ground and the towering plume of smoke streaking the northern sky.

Voices hushed into whispers, then into silence, until the only sound was the wind pushing through the grass. Djama lifted his staff. "Stand with your protector."

The mob shifted closer.

Noah felt them gathering behind him—children clutching their mothers' cloaks, elders leaning forward with sharp, knowing eyes, Big Red drawn tight around Little Red, whose tiny paws trembled.

Kirra stepped closer until her shoulder pressed against Noah's.
"We face it together," she whispered.

Steve planted himself just ahead of Noah, feathers razor-straight. "Let them come."

Frankie nodded, wide-eyed. "I mean... not literally right now, but... you know... bravely."

Wally simply said, "Noah's got us."

Noah looked at them all—his mob. His family. His reason. A warmth pulsed beneath his skin, matching the beat of his heart. His wings unfurled slightly, catching the firelight. The golden markings across his chest brightened in response to the land's call.

Djama's voice rose on the wind, ancient and steady:

"The boy is gone.
The protector stands."

And with that, Noah stepped forward—

Baan Marrung taking his place before his people.

The ridge overlooked the entire valley—every tree, every winding path, every breath of Country that Noah had ever known. It all stretched before him now, quiet and waiting, as if the land itself held its breath. He stepped forward, wings unfurling behind him in a sweep of golden brilliance. The energy rippled through the air, stirring dust, bending grass, pushing back the shadows that lingered at dawn's edge.

Djama stood behind him, staff planted firm. Kirra held Little Red's paw as Big Red leaned close, eyes soft with awe. Frankie and Wally huddled beside Steve—who stared north with the solemnity of someone who had seen this moment before. Far beyond the treeline, a new plume of smoke rose—thick, black, unnatural.

And between the drifting waves of pale mist... distorted silhouettes flickered:

Long red coats.
 White, hollow faces.
 Marching.

Kirra gripped Noah's arm. "It's starting." Noah didn't flinch. His wings lifted, catching the first rays of sunrise. Light poured across the ridge, washing over the mob, the camp, the land he belonged to.

Djama whispered, reverent, "Baan Marrung has risen."

Noah raised his head, eyes locked on the approaching threat.

"For my mob," he murmured.

"For this land."

He spread his wings—

And the protector answered the dawn.

THE LEGEND OF MARRĀKAI